BLACK WATER

BLACK WATER

WHITNEY SKOREYKO

First Edition, 2018

ISBN 978-1-9994033-0-0

Cover design by Fiona Jayde Media
Edited by Will Gabriel

To my family and friends.
Thank you for always supporting and encouraging me.

PROLOGUE

His shoes made impressions in the wet sand as he weaved between the rocks and driftwood. It was late—late enough that the sun was long gone, but not yet late enough to be early. He took in the fresh air, enjoyed sounds of the water, and tried to convince himself that his footsteps were steady enough that he could, in good conscience, return to his car and drive home. The numb buzz in his brain argued otherwise.

As he walked along the shoreline, he noticed a dark shape in the shallow water. It was too irregular to be a piece of fresh driftwood. He had a bad feeling, stopping briefly before he worked up the courage to approach the shape.

It was a man.

He sped his approach, soaking his shoes in the process. The bulk of a lifejacket caught his eye. He fished for the man's wrist and pulled it, dragging the man on his back. The wrist was cold, and the man wasn't breathing.

He stumbled backwards in shock.

Suddenly, he heard the snap of a dry branch echo from the trees near the concrete steps. He swung around, searching for the source of the noise. It was too dark to see more than the outline of the treeline. He abandoned the body and ran towards the path.

"Hey!" he shouted. "I've found . . . Someone drowned!" As he neared the path, he struck his shin on a large rock and tumbled to the sand.

As he recovered, he caught sight of a figure at the edge of the trees. It was a second man, but this one's shadowy posture was tight with rage, fists clenched. This man glanced between the body and the bystander. A heavy breath escaped his nose, and he started towards the bystander.

The first man shot up, darting towards the stairs back to his car. He tugged the handrail to heave himself up the stairs, only touching every third step. When he reached his car and grabbed the door handle, he spun around to get a glimpse of the man behind him in the flash of his tail lights.

But he wasn't followed.

PART ONE

CHAPTER ONE

Hannah looked at herself in the mirror. She could still see the loss in her eyes. She noticed that she had aged over the past year, but more than anything, she noticed pieces of her twin brother's face in her own. They had the same blue eyes, the same nose. When she smiled, which was rare these days, they had the same dimples.

Nearly a year had passed since Hunter's accident. She remembered the call like it was yesterday. She was at a medical gala having dinner with her colleagues when her phone rang. She thought it was a wrong number—a misdial—but it ended up being her worst nightmare.

She woke up almost every night since then soaked in sweat, sometimes screaming. The guilt made her ill. Hunter was supposed to be with her that night. He was supposed to be at the gala. When he didn't show up, she should have called. She should have known something was wrong.

For years, Hannah had been taking morning runs in the park near her home—the home she had once shared with Hunter. On the way back, she'd stop and sit on the beach, staring out at the ocean and the beautiful Victoria sky. Those visits had a different meaning now. They had found Hunter's body at that beach almost a year ago. Now, she'd sit and wonder how such a thing could happen to such a great person.

Hunter had been her rock. He was kind, genuine, and selfless. On their birthdays, he had always let her blow out the candles and open her gifts first. Hannah missed the fights they never had.

Hannah's thoughts stayed with Hunter as she finished getting ready for work, dreading this particular day without him. She stepped outside, locked the door, and pinched her arm.

Chapter Two

About fifteen minutes into her shift, Hannah was paged to emergency. She walked briskly through the double doors of the emergency department expecting a general plastics consult. Instead, she found her colleagues shouting, "Surprise!" with big smiles on their faces.

Tawn, her best friend and a fellow resident, was holding a white frosted cake bearing the words *Happy 29th Birthday*. An expensive cake, knowing Tawn.

"You're coming out with us tonight, my dear!" Tawn said with her typical bright smile.

Hannah faked a smile of her own. She was already weary from the thought of making small talk all day, and now she knew she would be doing it all night. But she knew if she refused, they would bug her about it for the rest of the day—and she had work to get done.

"Sounds great," Hannah said, wondering if she responded with the expected amount of enthusiasm.

With the birthday surprise over and done with, Hannah returned to her rounds. She tried to focus on her work and keep her mind off her painful memories, but the images and smells kept popping up in her head. She didn't know how much more of this day she could handle.

This was the first time she had to face their birthday alone. It didn't feel right. She paused at the charge desk, wanting more than anything to look over and see the jumbo box of chocolates he got her every year. They would be milk chocolate only—he knew her well—and he would write a little card with a pun he had thought up just for her.

Hannah wished she had appreciated those moments more when he was still alive.

She heard "Doctor Melbrook" over the paging system, and it snapped her out of her daydream. She knew that the more she focused on her work, the quicker the day would go. Then, after she played the part of the cheerful birthday girl for a couple of hours, the horrible, lonely day would be over. She patted the stethoscope around her neck and headed for the elevators.

Hannah hit the button for the third floor and looked out into the lobby just in time to see a tall man with dark brown hair approach the elevator. When their eyes locked, he froze and gazed at her intently. She felt a shiver down her spine. As he stared, the doors closed, and the elevator started moving.

Is there something on my face? Hannah pulled her phone out of her pocket and checked herself in the camera. Nothing unusual to be seen—just the same dark circles under her tired eyes.

* * *

After work, Hannah went straight home. As she pulled into the driveway, she noticed a red object sitting on her doorstep. She grabbed her bag, got out of her car, and walked up the driveway towards the door. When she realized what was sitting there, she froze. She didn't know whether she should scream or cry. She picked up the familiar box of chocolates and opened the lid. There were only milk chocolates inside. The small card attached to the lid showed a picture of an arm bone sticking out of a cake. It read, *Happy Birthday, Hannah! Hope you find this humerus.*

CHAPTER THREE

Hannah dropped the box and stared at it. She could feel her heart beating hard in her chest. She didn't understand what to make of this. Was it some sort of cruel joke?

She glanced around her front yard. Then, steeling herself, she took the box into her house, dropping it on the coffee table and slumping onto the couch. She waited for her heart to slow down. That box—that card . . . She felt a tear run down her cheek. Her mind was running a hundred miles a minute.

After a few minutes, a thought surfaced. She still had it, didn't she?

She went to her garage and pulled a large plastic bin out from the bottom shelf. Inside the bin was a large red box. She wiped her eyes with her wrist. That box of chocolates and the ring on her right hand were the last things he had given her before he died.

Hannah took the box to her living room and set it down next to its twin. This box was lighter—only a few lonely chocolates remained at the bottom—but it was otherwise identical. She stared at the boxes for what felt like an hour.

Suddenly, her phone rang, and Hannah jumped.

"Hello?" she said. She could barely hold the phone steady to her ear.

"Hey girl, will you be ready to go soon?" Tawn asked.

Hannah could not focus. She just kept her eyes peeled on the large red boxes in front of her.

"Hannah? Are you there?"

She realized she was being asked a question. "Yeah, I just need to change and freshen up and I'll be ready to go." Hannah didn't recognize her voice as she spoke. It sounded lost and afraid. She pulled her eyes away from the boxes and tried to gather her composure.

"Great!" Tawn said. "I'm on my way, so I'll see you soon. Can't wait to celebrate your big day with you tonight!"

Hannah only had ten or fifteen minutes before Tawn would arrive, and she didn't want Tawn to come inside. The chocolates had to be a secret for now. Tawn would freak out and tell her brother, who was a police officer. Hannah couldn't handle the questions and the attention—not today.

She rushed to her closet to grab an outfit. It was black from top to bottom: a dress with long lace sleeves, a pair of black tights, and heel booties.

Hannah went to the mirror, dabbed her eyes with a tissue, touched up her light makeup, and combed her straight blonde hair with her fingers. An outsider would probably see what she used to see in the mirror: a slim, young, beautiful woman. Hannah still only saw the face of her twin brother.

She grabbed her purse off the counter and glanced again at the chocolates sitting on the coffee table. She didn't know how she would make it through the night.

Hannah heard a honk from outside. She stepped out the door, locked it behind her, and pinched her arm.

Hannah hopped into the passenger side of Tawn's Acura. If her anxiety and discomfort weren't already bad enough, the hot leather seat made things worse. She tried to hide her misery as she greeted Tawn.

Hannah looked over at Tawn and her outfit. She was wearing a white dress with cap sleeves and a hemline just above her knees. The dress contrasted well with Tawn's olive skin and her long, dark brown, well-maintained hair. Beautiful as always, but Tawn took full advantage of her freedom from her monochrome scrubs. Hannah had once asked Tawn why she spent so much money on her appearance when she lived in a dingy studio apartment. Tawn replied, *Only a few people are lucky enough to see my place. Everyone gets to see me.*

Tawn turned to Hannah when they hit a red light. "You're okay, right?"

"Yeah—I'm fine."

"Well, get ready to feel even better. We're going to have a blast!" Tawn said.

"Can't wait," Hannah replied. "Thanks again for planning this."

"Are you kidding, girl? It's no problem at all! We all love spending time with you. It's been too long since you came out with us after work."

She was right. Hannah had been especially withdrawn for the past year. Going out and having fun felt wrong somehow. She would catch herself smiling and would instantly feel guilty.

"It's a great bar, too," Tawn continued. "A *lot* of cute guys."

Hannah didn't reply to this. Instead, she remembered the man she saw in the hospital lobby. He *was* quite handsome, looking back. Hannah caught herself wishing she had held the elevator door open for him.

At the bar, Hannah spotted their table in seconds. There were balloons, a couple of gift bags, and about a dozen of her friends and colleagues sitting there waiting for her to arrive. They all greeted her with hugs and smiles. Hannah made her rounds to thank everyone for coming and then found her spot in the middle of the table next to Tawn and Adam. Adam picked at the label on his beer and glanced around the room.

Adam worked as a cardiology resident at the same hospital. He had been a close friend of Hunter's. He and Hannah used to be close, too. One night, when Hannah had joined him and Hunter on their yearly trip to the mountains, they became *very* close. It was apparently a mistake. A couple of weeks later, Adam backed off hard and had acted weird around her ever since.

Still, Hannah thought Adam was handsome. He was tall with blonde hair and blue eyes like hers. He was active and in shape. He was kind and had always looked out for her and her brother.

The waitress came shortly after Hannah sat down. Hannah was thankful for the quick service—she really needed a drink.

"What can I get for the birthday girl?"

"I'll have a pint of your lightest beer with a lime wedge, please."

Hannah was always picked on by her friends for still being a beer drinker at the age of twenty-nine. But she liked what she liked, and Hannah rarely broke any habits.

Two pints later, Hannah got up to use the washroom. The bar was getting crowded, and the DJ was just setting up. She almost tripped while trying to walk over his cords in her high heels. Hannah had always been a bit of a lightweight and was finding herself feeling a bit tipsy.

When she went to wash her hands, she stared at herself in the mirror. She saw him in her face again. Her heart ached as she studied the little details of her face that matched his.

She snapped herself out of it and remembered that the night out was being held in honour of her birthday. A lot of people went out of their way to be there for her. She freshened up her makeup and straightened her dress over her black tights.

Hannah was heading back to the table when she saw something that stopped her dead in her tracks. It was the man again. He was sitting at the bar, staring at her with his deep green eyes. His gaze was just as intense as it had been that morning. But this time, he wore a smile.

Chapter Four

Was he an old patient? Had he done work on her home? None of this seemed right, but why else did he seem to know her? Her heart was racing as she approached him at the bar. It was like her legs were on autopilot. All she could hear was her loud breathing and her heart pounding in her chest. Despite herself, she admired his closely cropped facial hair, his perfect bone structure, and his glowing, tanned skin. Hannah suddenly felt self-conscious about her hastily assembled outfit.

As she got closer, he pulled out the chair next to him and signalled for her to join him. She sat down, and he slid a shot glass in front of her.

"Happy Birthday, Hannah," the man said, his eyes piercing into her soul.

Hannah flinched. "How did you know it was my birthday?" *And how does he know my name?*

"I'm stalking you," he replied.

Hannah felt her mouth drop open. She didn't know what to say.

The man grimaced a little. "Bad joke? Sorry. I overheard some people wishing you happy birthday when you came in."

Hannah smiled, relieved, and fiddled with the ring on her right middle finger.

He took the shot to his mouth and lifted his empty glass in the air. She gazed into his eyes, then did the same.

He smiled briefly, gave another grimace, then pulled his phone out of his pocket. Looking at the screen, he got up from the bar-stool. "Sorry. Gotta go."

He grabbed his wallet and, before he got too far, looked back directly into her eyes. "See you, Hannah." He winked and headed towards the door.

Hannah somehow knew this was not going to be the last time she saw this man.

At least, she hoped not.

CHAPTER FIVE

Hannah didn't stay much longer, despite her friends' protests. She gathered her gifts, said her goodbyes, and called an Uber.

Back at home, she immediately peeled off her black tights—the humid heat made them stick to her legs. She was starting to sober up. She poured herself a big glass of water and headed towards her bedroom. As she walked down the hall, she stopped right outside the spare bedroom. It was still just as he left it. Hannah hadn't intended to leave his things untouched, but it was too hard to pack him away for good.

She entered the spare room and sat on the bed. The sheets were soft and cool against her thighs. She regarded Hunter's scattered things, wondering what her parents would have done with his room if he had still lived with them.

Her mother would have probably wanted to pack everything away. It seemed she had moved on after Hunter's death—aggressively, in fact. She hardly had an evening that wasn't booked with some club meeting or social outing.

Hannah's father? Who knows what he'd have wanted to do with Hunter's things. He sold his stake in his fishing boat rental business and retreated with Hannah's mother to the mainland. Hannah had no idea what he did those days. She could never keep him on the phone for long.

Hannah caught herself in a daze, daydreaming about the past. She felt left behind, as if Hunter's death had knocked her out of the world's rhythm and she never found her place again. She left the room and decided tonight was not going to be the night she would sort through her brother's things. She was just not ready to let him go.

Hannah walked into her bedroom and closed the blinds. She put on her pajamas and then went to the master bathroom to brush her teeth.

Hannah couldn't help but remember the box of chocolates. She could not think of a single person who would do something like that to her. The person who wrote the card knew what kind of thing Hunter would have written. This person knew she was a doctor. They knew where she lived.

She tried to put it out of her mind and focus on just getting some sleep. Deep down, she was terrified. She wished her brother was there to protect her.

She crawled into her bed and stared up at her ceiling. The small skylight right above her bed was a small comfort. Ever since she was a child, Hannah had felt drawn to the sky. Almost every night when she was young, she would beg her father to sit outside with her before bedtime, and they would watch the stars together while lying in the grass. For her thirteenth birthday he bought her a telescope. Hannah never forgot the first time she saw the night sky up close. The stars looked like diamonds and the moon lit up her spirit.

Hannah's mind was racing. It had been an overwhelming night. She thought about the man at the bar. She thought about her friends—wondered if they could pick up on the fact that she was hurting inside. Somewhere lost in her thoughts, she fell asleep.

That night, Hannah dreamt of a boat. As it approached where she sat on the shoreline, she noticed it was much larger than she had thought. It was more of a large yacht. She sat in the sand and watched it sail closer to her. As she sat in the darkness, she could begin to make out figures of people through the glass windows. They seemed happy and relaxed. She saw crystal chandeliers hanging from the ceiling and champagne glasses in their hands. She watched a woman tip her head back and laugh, but she couldn't make out who or what she was laughing at. The ship was surrounded by darkness with an endless wake trailing behind it. Hannah could not take her eyes away from the ship.

The boat continued to approach her. The woman she had seen in the window was now standing out on the deck, facing Hannah. She had one hand on the railing and her other on her glass of champagne. She was wearing a white gown, and Hannah could see from afar that she was beautiful. She pulled her hand up from the railing and blew a kiss. Hannah felt confused. She looked to see if there was anyone else on the beach, but it was just her alone in the darkness.

Suddenly the boat picked up speed, uninhibited by the shallows near the shore. Hannah was scared, but she was stuck in place. As she wriggled ineffectually, she felt something touching the side of her foot. She looked down and saw the jumbo box of chocolates. The ground underneath it shook as the ship tore through the rocks and sand. She looked up, and just as the ship was about to hit her, she woke up screaming.

Hannah was soaked in sweat. *That dream again*, she thought. *But that's the first time the ship got so close.*

Slivers of daylight were already streaming through her blinds. She got up and put on her housecoat.

Hannah walked out into the living room and sat across from the two boxes of chocolates. That part hadn't been a dream after all. She studied the new card for a good twenty minutes, comparing it with the one on the year-old box. *It even has the same writing.*

Hannah had a full four days off for the first time in three

months. They insisted she take the weekend off so she could stay up late and celebrate for her birthday. She had planned on calling in on Saturday to pick up extra shifts, as she usually would, but instead she decided she needed time to process all of this. Still, Hannah felt like she needed to get out of her house. There were too many memories there.

She went to her bedroom and grabbed a black tank top off the floor. She opened her bottom dresser drawer and picked up the first pair of jean shorts she saw. She went to the front door and slipped on her flip-flops. She grabbed her phone and her wallet and put them in her purse. Then, she stepped out, locked the door, and pinched her arm.

CHAPTER SIX

Hannah decided to walk the fifteen minutes to the café and grab breakfast. Whenever she and Hunter had worked the same shift, they would drive together and stop at the café on the way to the hospital. She always got a black tea with one cream and one sweetener, and he would get a hazelnut latte. He would say to her every morning that she needed to change it up and live a little, but Hannah was always known to be a creature of habit.

She walked slowly, paying more attention to her surroundings and the people of her neighbourhood than usual. Every time she noticed a vaguely familiar face, she'd think, *Could that be who left the chocolates?*

As she walked by the outdoor patio of the café, she wondered why no one was sitting outside. As she opened the door, she was greeted by the answer: a relieving wave of cool, conditioned air. Hannah had been so distracted on her walk that she hadn't realized she was sweating.

She ordered a piece of banana bread and paused before ordering her drink. "And a large hazelnut latte, please." Hannah felt her eyes well up as she made her small tribute to Hunter. She willed the tears to stay back, accepted her brown-bagged banana bread, and stepped away from the counter to wait for her coffee.

A minute later, the barista shouted, "Hazelnut latte for Hunter!"

Hannah faced the woman, wide-eyed.

The barista flushed. "I'm sorry, dear, it must have reminded me of . . . I'm really sorry." She handed the latte to Hannah and averted her eyes.

Hannah took her drink, thankful that at least one person in the café couldn't see the tears that had betrayed her. She hurried outside and sat at a patio table where she would be out of view from the inside.

Hannah sat there for a few minutes, dabbing her eyes with a napkin, before she had calmed down enough to eat. As she took bites of her banana bread and sipped her latte, she watched the people coming and going on the bike path across the road. There were all sorts of families and couples. Occasionally, she would notice someone walking alone and wondered if they felt as lonely and empty inside as she did. She wondered if they had ever lost someone close to them. She wouldn't have wished that feeling of loss on anyone.

Eventually, Hannah surprised herself with a faint smile. The man from the night before had managed to slip into the forefront of her thoughts again. She couldn't quite put her finger on it—why he had such an impact on her. It wasn't uncommon for men to approach Hannah and flirt with her a little, even when she was working in her scrubs and white doctor's coat, but she hadn't reacted this way in a year.

She kept trying to push him out of her thoughts, but he wouldn't go away. She could see his perfect tanned skin and his strong, sculpted cheekbones. It couldn't just be a coincidence that he appeared at the hospital and then again at the bar in the same day, could it? And on her birthday, of all nights? Or did he know she was going to be there?

Hannah decided her thoughts weren't getting her anywhere. She finished the last sip of her latte and peeled her sticky thighs off the seat.

Hannah decided to walk through the park on the way back home. She walked across the road and onto the paved path surrounded by trees. As she walked, she felt her pocket vibrate. Tawn's name appeared on the screen of her phone. She answered on the second ring.

"Hey Tawn," Hannah said.

"Hey girl! Did you have the best time last night?"

"Yeah, it was great going out with you guys! Thanks again for putting it together." Hannah felt awkward about her artificially cheerful words, but she always felt some sort of obligation to match Tawn's level of enthusiasm.

Tawn paused for a moment and then asked a question she must have been holding in all morning, bypassing the stream of "Tawn things" she usually indulged in before asking a thing about Hannah. "So . . . How about that cute guy you were talking to at the bar last night?" Hannah thought there might have been a little jealousy in Tawn's voice.

She wondered about the answer to that question herself. She didn't know quite how to respond. "He was just some random guy."

"Oh, I thought maybe you guys were hitting it off. It seemed like he was into you."

Hannah could tell that Tawn was disappointed with her response, but she didn't have anything more to say about him. She didn't know anything about him, though she wished she did.

"Well, anyways, I just wanted to make sure that you were having a good day today. I know yesterday must have been hard. I'm proud of you for coming out. Let me know if you need anything at all."

"Thanks, Tawn. You're the best."

Before she hung up, Tawn extended another invite: "Hey, by the way, some of us are going out to the club tonight. We're going to start the party off at Adrianna's and head to the bar from there. Don't tell me you already have plans—I know you don't!"

Good old Tawn.

"I'll think about it and let you know later," said Hannah.

That seemed to be enough for Tawn. Hannah pulled the phone away from her ear and hung up. She thought about the guy from the night before and realized she was disappointed herself—she didn't even know his name. She wished she would have asked it and wondered if she would ever get to look into his green eyes again.

CHAPTER SEVEN

Back at home, Hannah couldn't sit still. She paced, wrung her hands, and cleaned things that didn't need cleaning. The empty house—and the boxes of chocolate still sitting on her coffee table—gave her little peace and comfort. Eventually, she decided that for once she would go out with her friends without being forced to join them.

She texted Tawn then went to her closet to find an outfit. She went with all black again: black converse sneakers with white laces, black jeans, and a band shirt with a grey skull on the front.

As she straightened her blonde hair, she noticed how long it was getting. She tried to recall the last time she had cut it and realized it had been more than a year ago—when he was still alive. It was a few inches past her shoulders now and full of split ends.

When she got into the Uber, Hannah thought about how long it had been since she last went to Adrianna's place. She saw Adrianna plenty in medical school. She saw her less when they took internships at different hospitals. She saw her less still when Hannah had practically stopped going out altogether. Adrianna was always a big personality, and so were a lot of her friends, so Hannah worried she would barely fit in anymore.

On her breaks at work, she still checked on the social media accounts of her friends and co-workers. But as her social circles continued to grow and develop, Hannah felt more distant from them than ever.

Before she knew it, the Uber had dropped her off at Adrianna's. Hannah walked up to the door and took a deep breath to collect herself before ringing the doorbell.

Hannah watched through the glass window as Tawn practically ran to answer the door. Tawn flung the door open and hugged her tightly. Hannah could smell the alcohol on her friend's breath.

"I'm so glad you came!" Tawn shouted, high-pitched enough to make Hannah flinch a little. "I have a special surprise for you!"

Hannah wondered what Tawn could possibly have in store for her. She wouldn't have had much time to prepare a surprise with only an hour's warning.

"What is it?" Hannah asked.

Tawn grabbed Hannah's hand and practically dragged her into the kitchen. Hannah saw a group of old acquaintances and a few strangers around the island drinking champagne. She had a flashback to her dream the night before and remembered the woman holding the glass of champagne in the moonlight. Then, she saw Adam looking out into the backyard, his arm around another man's shoulder.

Hannah knew it was him. She had chills and could feel her heart racing. She didn't take her eyes off him as he and Adam turned and separated. He had broad shoulders and lean, long legs, covered by a well-fitted collared shirt and dark grey pants. She could see the outline of his muscles even under his clothing. Hannah blushed as she caught herself noticing these things.

He smiled as he made eye contact with her. Hannah walked across the kitchen towards him and Adam. She felt like her body and her mind had been disconnected. She was physically moving but mentally felt frozen in time. She could feel a strong energy pulling her in his direction, and there was nothing she could do to stop it.

Adam put his hands in his pockets and broke the silence.

"Hannah, I guess you've met Luke." He tipped his head towards the man as he spoke.

Hannah played with the ring on her right hand. "Yes, we met last night. Sorry, I forgot to ask your name," she said as she looked in his eyes.

"Well, now you know—and I hope you won't forget," he replied, returning an intense gaze.

Adam retreated out onto the patio with his beer.

"Hannah!" said Adrianna from behind the island. "Have some champagne!" She brought Hannah a glass with raspberries at the bottom.

"Yeah . . . Thanks, Adrianna. Good to see you." She barely took her eyes off Luke as she spoke.

"Want to go outside?" Luke asked.

"Sure," she answered as she followed him out the sliding door. Hannah felt like she was in a dream.

On the patio, a few guys—now including Adam—sat around the table or leaned against the patio railing. A few more people lazed in the hot tub near the foot of the stairs, a half-empty bottle and a scattering of shot glasses nearby.

Hannah and Luke took a pair of empty chairs at the table. Hannah felt nervous and excited.

Soon, Luke had been dragged into a conversation about sports. The other guys nodded appreciatively at his words. It seemed he really knew his stuff. Hannah sat quietly drinking her champagne—faster than she would have liked to. Still, Luke never seemed to forget Hannah was there. He would regularly glance at her and smile, occasionally losing his place in the conversation.

Just when the others had begun to filter back into the house, Adrianna came out into the yard to say that the limo had arrived. Everyone tossed back their drinks and grabbed their things. Luke offered his hand to help Hannah from her chair, and they made their way through the sliding door. Luke grazed her back with his hand to guide her inside. His touch made her body tingle. She couldn't help but notice the strong hold he had on her, despite the fact that they had only met the day before—and that she had only learned his name a half hour ago.

She noticed he was no longer near her when she stepped into the limo. She took the seat across from Adam, leaving a space next to herself for Luke. When he arrived, he was carrying a pair of freshly-opened beers. He handed one to Hannah and sat beside her.

His leg was touching hers. She could feel her stomach turning and her heart racing. *How does he know I'm a beer drinker?*

"Thanks," she said.

He lifted his bottle and clinked it against hers. "Cheers."

They both tilted their bottles back. Hannah could feel the alcohol going straight to her head. She had eaten barely anything all day and was starting to regret it.

"So how do you know Adrianna?" Hannah asked him.

"I met some of your friends last night after you left." His eyes were playful, and she wasn't quite sure what they were trying to tell her.

Hannah was confused. She thought he had left after he walked away from her at the bar. She would have stayed longer if she had known he was still there.

He put his hand on her thigh. She was startled by the gesture, but she loved the feeling of him touching her, and she couldn't pull herself away.

"I feel like I've known you forever." He was so confident when he spoke.

Hannah believed it—he was sure confident enough, and it was winning her over in a big way. Still, she was surprised. She had been worried she might never see him again, even though they had just met, and yet there he was.

She had felt a powerful feeling towards him the moment she saw him in the hospital lobby. She felt it again when she saw him that same night. She felt it now too as she looked into his eyes. Nobody had given her that feeling in a long time. Nobody had been able to make her forget the emptiness. The grief. Herself.

When the limo stopped at the club, everyone walked to the front of the line. They were with Adrianna, and most of them knew what that meant: no lines. She refused to wait, so she would never go anywhere before she found out how to get on the guest list.

"Hey, Hannah," Adam said, leaning towards her. "It's good to see you come out like this." He looked like he was searching for more to say, but nothing else came.

Further casual conversation was drowned out by the heavy bass and the buzz of voices as they entered the darkened club. Adrianna grabbed Tawn and another friend by the wrist and pulled them towards the dance floor. She turned and shouted to Hannah. "Come on!"

"Maybe later," Hannah shouted back, mouthing the words clearly in case she wasn't heard. Then Hannah, Luke, and Adam made their way to the nearest bartender.

Hannah ordered a light beer, and Adam surprised her by putting it on his tab. Was it jealousy? That didn't seem right. Adam had been distant for so long.

The three of them took a seat at a small table near the bar. Hannah and Luke exchanged short sentences over the noise while Adam downed his beer quickly. Peeling the label on his empty bottle, he waited for them to half finish theirs then offered to buy another round. Luke seemed ready to protest, but he gave up once Adam's back was turned.

Luke turned back to Hannah. "What's the deal between you and Adam?"

"Oh, it's nothing," Hannah said. "We're just friends." She caught herself combing her fingers through her hair, hoping Luke didn't pry. She squirmed a little and realized she needed to use the washroom. "I'll be right back," she shouted, leaving her purse on the table to prove she wasn't running away.

Hannah moved past the dance floor, waving to Tawn, and finally made it to the back of the club where the restrooms were located. She walked down the dark hallway and entered the ladies room.

When she finished, Hannah looked at herself in the mirror and regretted leaving her purse behind. Her makeup could have used a touch-up, and she wished she had a piece of gum. She tamed her hair the best she could. She hadn't cared so much about what she looked like for a long time. It felt so foreign.

When she returned to the table, Hannah saw Adam sitting alone with three beers. There was no trace of Luke.

"He had to go," Adam said, taking a swig. He pushed a bottle towards Hannah's seat and nodded.

Hannah frowned and gestured the bottle away. *What's Adam's problem?*

Anger was quickly replaced with worry. She had her second chance with Luke, and now it was gone. Would she even get a third?

Without a word, Hannah grabbed her purse and headed for the door.

CHAPTER EIGHT

When Hannah got home, she was exhausted. She kicked off her shoes at the door and headed straight for her bedroom. She almost made it to her room, but she stopped when she saw his things. She needed company—even from someone who wasn't there anymore. Hannah pushed the spare room door the rest of the way open and slowly walked inside.

She thought about how she used to come home late and find him sitting on the edge of his bed playing his acoustic guitar. It had always amazed her how good he was. His technique was raw, lacking any formal training, but he had a talent for making you feel the music. She would come to the doorway of his room, he would stop, and she would tell him about her night. He would just listen patiently as if nothing else mattered.

She sat in his place, grabbing a hoodie that hung on the bedpost and bringing it up to her nose. She thought she could still smell his cologne on it. Then, she stared at the nightstand where he had kept his journal.

Hunter had started keeping a journal during his year off between undergraduate studies and med school. While Hannah pushed straight on through, Hunter travelled, spending six months in Australia and New Zealand then moving on to Germany and

England for the remainder of his time away. He must have gotten all the adventurer genes, Hannah always thought.

She opened the drawer, and there it sat next to a pair of guitar picks and a watch he never wore. *Hunter Melbrook, 2017*, read the cover. It had an eerie quality of a gravestone.

The temptation to read it had always been there, but Hannah could never bring herself to do it. This time, she needed his words more than ever. As soon as she opened the journal and saw his writing, a tear streamed down her cheek. She flipped to August 26th. Empty, of course. He never went home that night. As a tear hit the page, Hannah flipped back to the beginning and read.

January 1, 2017

I forgot to write yesterday, so I should go over that before I move on. First things first: my resolution for this year is to get my own place. Don't get me wrong, I love living with Hannah, but sometimes I think we both need our own space. Plus, I'm making a bit more money now as a resident, and I think Hannah's ready to be independent.

I managed to go out for New Years last night, which is the first time in a while that I've been able to enjoy myself and take my mind off the job. Adam hosted his annual New Years Eve party. It was a fun night, but something strange happened on the way home that I can't shake. As I got out of my cab, I saw a man watching me from the open window of his car across the street. It sure didn't seem like the curiosity of a random stranger. His gaze followed me as I walked. It was dark outside, so I couldn't quite make out his face, but he drove a black BMW coupe and it looked to me like he was wearing a suit.

Who knows, maybe I just had too much to drink, but that guy gave me the creeps.

Anyway, today I went on my yearly hike with Adam and Patrick. As usual, it was really cold and a little miserable, but hey, it's tradition.

Two things stuck out in Hannah's mind. First of all, Hannah was surprised Hunter had planned on moving out. He hadn't told her anything about that. She knew they wouldn't have lived together forever, but when had he planned on telling her?

Second, and more ominous, was the man who had been watching Hunter from outside of her home. Maybe it was nothing, but it gave Hannah a feeling she couldn't shake.

Hannah flipped ahead to read another entry, hoping to find something a little more reassuring.

February 22, 2017

I'm starting to feel like I'm living in the Twilight Zone. Every day feels the same. My scheduled shifts are still nothing but scut work, and I still get stuck with it when I volunteer for more hours. I don't know how I'm ever going to break out of this. How can I get my attending to trust me? I look at Hannah and see how well she's doing and how respected she is. Did she ever have as hard a time as I'm having? Or am I just unlucky? Either way, I need to get out of this rut. My family has high expectations of me, and I don't want to let them down.

Maybe I just had a really bad day, but I don't feel like I've had a great one in a long time. The long hours are killer, and I'm still not sleeping well. At least tomorrow night I get to meet up with some friends. Hopefully that makes me feel better.

How had Hannah not seen that her brother was feeling that way? He was always positive and came across as so put together. Hannah had looked up to him in so many ways. He was kind and patient and he never treated her like she was the annoying sister. They were friends.

Hannah was having a bad day of her own, and now she just wanted it to be over. She closed the journal, put it back in Hunter's nightstand, and dragged herself to bed.

CHAPTER NINE

When Hannah awoke, it was ten in the morning. She vaguely remembered having the boat dream again, but it wasn't until she stepped out of the shower that she remembered another detail: a man staring at her from a black BMW. She got dressed and went to Hunter's room to read that passage again.

As soon as she grabbed the journal, Hannah heard her doorbell ring. She practically jumped out of her skin. Tossing the journal on the couch as she passed by, she went to answer the door.

It was Tawn, smiling and holding pair of coffees and a paper bag. Hannah knew just what was in the bag: bagels. Tawn was clearly trying to revive their old morning-after tradition where they'd have breakfast together and gossip about the night before.

"You're home!" Tawn said. "I was worried you'd still be . . . *out*."

"Where else would I be?" Hannah said as she glanced around her living room. The chocolates and the journal were in plain sight. She quickly directed Tawn through the house and out to the deck.

"Don't play dumb with me, Hannah. You went home with him, didn't you? Or is he *here?*" Tawn glanced back into the house behind her.

"With Luke? No." *But I probably would have*, she thought.

They sat at the table, and Hannah rolled the umbrella up to shield them from the hot sun. Tawn handed Hannah a bagel and a coffee.

"But you left together, right?"

"I left after he did. We talked for a while, then I went to the bathroom. When I got back, he was gone."

A concerned look ran across Tawn's face. "That's so weird. He seemed really into you. What could have happened?"

Hannah thought about this for a moment. She suspected Adam had something to do with it, but she didn't think it was fair to involve Tawn. The two were friends, after all.

Instead, she just shrugged.

Tawn shook her head. "Maybe it was some sort of emergency. If not, he's an idiot. A *hot* idiot"—Hannah smiled at this—"but still an idiot. Anyways, you should have stayed! It was a lot of fun."

Tawn and Hannah spent the next hour recapping the evening from Tawn's perspective. Tawn apparently met a guy from Germany and they ended up spending most of the night dancing together and making out. She told Hannah about how much of a gentleman he was and how he planned on taking her out for dinner on Tuesday. Hannah knew better than to get attached to any of Tawn's boyfriends or potential prospects. She was a bit pessimistic in that regard, but she had seen Tawn fall into the same pattern time and time again. She would meet a guy and get attached too quickly, he would do something miniscule to disappoint her, and she would end it. Hannah was starting to worry about Tawn's impossible expectations.

"Hey," Tawn said as she was standing to leave, "what happened to your ring?"

Hannah looked down at her right hand—the hand where she kept the ring Hunter gave her—gave her on their twenty-seventh birthday. It was gone.

"I don't know, maybe I . . . Maybe I left it in my locker." Hannah tried to remember if she had worn it since Friday. Surely she would have noticed it missing by now.

"Well, I'm sure it'll turn up," Tawn said. She hugged Hannah goodbye and let herself out.

CHAPTER TEN

With Tawn gone, Hannah called the hospital to cut her time off short. She hated the idea of spending the next two days idle, and she wanted to see if she really had left the ring at work. As usual, they were happy to schedule her for the next day.

Hannah dropped onto the couch, landing right next to Hunter's journal. She remembered she had meant to read it before Tawn arrived, but she couldn't remember why. She opened the journal and turned to the second page.

January 2, 2017

My attending has to be the toughest doctor at the hospital. I was sure he'd go easier on me once I was no longer an intern, but it still feels like he's just waiting for me to mess up. Hannah is so lucky she has it easy.

No, that's not fair. Hannah works hard. It's just disheartening to see her go about her job with such confidence when I can't seem to impress anyone.

There's always a trade-off, I guess. I know Hannah can't cook to save her life. I should probably teach her a thing or two before I get my own place. Wouldn't do to leave her dependent on takeout and frozen dinners.

Hannah had no idea her brother had been struggling. He hid it well—or maybe Hannah just hadn't paid enough attention.

Either way, Hunter had been right about her lack of skills in the kitchen. She remembered he *had* tried to teach her a little. The results were disappointing. Before long, she quit trying altogether.

Hannah remembered that her stores of protein bars and microwaveable meals were getting low, so she decided to go grocery shopping. But before she could put the journal down, she spotted the boxes of chocolates again. *What was he thinking the day before he died?*

She opened to the last page he had used.

August 25, 2017

I don't know why he wants to meet on a cruise ship, and I know it's stupid of me to agree to do it, but I need to sort this out once and for all. I need to know what he wants; I can't go on wondering if he'll be out there watching me for the rest of my life. This is my chance to get everything back to normal.

I don't want to worry Nicole, so I'll just have to apologize later. She was looking forward to meeting Hannah tomorrow, but it can wait a day.

Hannah found her jaw clenching tightly. This was too much. A cruise ship? A stalker? Was it the same man from before, or was it someone else?

And this Nicole. Who was she? How long had Hunter been seeing someone without telling her? Hannah had never kept any secrets from him, and she was surprised he had so many.

She tossed the journal to the floor, grabbed her purse, and headed straight to her car.

Hannah usually dreaded going to the grocery store. She couldn't stand all the people and carts left in the aisles, and she would always come home in a bad mood. Still, she never took long. Hannah did most of her shopping in the freezer aisle and meal replacement section. So, not even an hour after she left home, Hannah was loading her bags into the back of her car.

After she buckled herself in, Hannah decided she would call her parents. She preferred to call them on the drive home from work or errands. That way, she'd always have a good excuse to hang up after fifteen or twenty minutes. It had been awkward talking to them since Hunter died. Her mother was always going on about her book club or her dance class or her exercise groups—she never asked Hannah about her life anymore. Her father, on the other hand, was completely checked out. It was a struggle to get him to say anything at all.

As Hannah scrolled through her contacts, she noticed something. It was *his* number—two entries above *Mom and Dad*. His name stood out to her like blood on a white wall. *How did he get his number in my phone without me knowing about it?*

Hannah had butterflies in her stomach. She put off her call to her parents and thought about Luke the entire drive home. Maybe she hadn't missed her chance after all. As unusual as it was to get his number like that, it meant he was still interested, right?

When she got home, Hannah unloaded her groceries while debating whether she should text him. She wanted to, but she wished he would be the one to reach out to her instead.

Hannah cracked open a beer as she entertained the idea of reaching out to him. Before she knew it, she was on her second. Finally, she worked up the courage to text him.

Hannah: Did I scare you away yesterday?

Hannah anxiously sipped her second beer as she waited for her phone to buzz in response. It felt like an eternity. Hannah was starting to get desperate and wondered what he could possibly be up to. Finally, her phone vibrated and lit up on the counter.

Luke: No, not at all. I just had somewhere I needed to be. I see you found my number ;)

Hannah: I'm not sure how you pulled it off but somehow it found its way into my contact list.

Hannah blushed as she imagined him smiling at her messages.

Luke: Can I come by your place tonight? I have something for you.

Hannah read and reread his text. *Here? Tonight?* She was nervous about the thought of him being in her house. They had only spoken twice. Still, she so badly wanted to see him. She craved his presence and the way he made her feel. She thought about it for several minutes, imagining what the visit might be like.

Finally, she texted him her address.

Hannah: I'll be home at 7.

Luke: Great, see you then.

It was still late afternoon, but Hannah didn't want to seem as desperate to see him as she really was. Plus, her little white lie gave her a chance to get ready—and maybe have another beer to calm her nerves.

Hannah spent more time putting herself together than she had in a long time. She agonized over her outfit, did her makeup with an unusual amount of care, and touched up her hair with a straightener.

Once she was satisfied with her appearance, she shifted her focus to the house. She tidied up as thoroughly as possible and tossed the boxes of chocolates onto Hunter's bed. She then returned to the living room for the journal, placed it next to the chocolates, and closed the door as she left. She stood with her back pressed to the door for a few minutes. The thoughts rushed in as she thought about the journal. She tried to push them out. She wanted to know more about the cruise ship, about the man Hunter was meeting with, and about Nicole—but she didn't have the time. *Not tonight*, she thought.

Halfway down the hallway, Hannah paused. She turned back, retrieved the journal, and went to secure it in her own nightstand.

Hannah pulled out her laptop and sat on her bed. By then, she only had minutes before Luke was to arrive, but she wanted to know more about him. She opened her Facebook page and typed *Luke* into the search bar. That was no help—there must have been hundreds of Lukes in Victoria, and she didn't know his last name.

She decided to try a different tack: maybe Adam, Adrianna, or Tawn had added him during the previous two evenings. But before she could check, there was a knock at the front door.

Her stomach turned. She walked slowly to the door, but her chest heaved as if she had been running. Her hands were clammy as she turned the doorknob.

The second she saw his face, her heart skipped a beat. He looked even more handsome than he had the night before. He was clean-shaven this time. Hannah imagined the feeling of his smooth face on her own. Then, she imagined it elsewhere.

He smiled, leaning on Hannah's doorframe. "Are you going to invite me in, or would you just like to hang out on your front porch?"

"Right." Hannah laughed and gestured for him to follow her inside. She wondered if he could hear her breathing—if he noticed her chest rising and falling heavily. She was so intimidated by that man.

"Here," he said, handing her a small, black gift bag. She had no clue what he could have possibly gotten for her. They barely knew each other. It was strange enough that he was there in her house when they had only known each other for a couple of days. Her friends would probably think she was mad if they found out she let a virtual stranger over. Well, *some* of them wouldn't. But Hannah wasn't normally like that.

Hannah felt self-conscious as Luke watched her reach into the bag. She tucked the tissue paper back and pulled out a silver chain necklace. Hannah inhaled sharply. On the necklace was a silver ring bearing a sapphire surrounded by two small diamonds.

It was the most important gift she had ever received—that is, it already had been. It was *her ring*.

Luke grabbed it and signalled for her to turn around. He put the necklace around her neck and did up the clasp. Hannah held the ring in her fingers.

"Where did you find this? And how did you know it was mine?" Hannah asked.

"I saw you fiddling with it at the bar the other night. I think you must have been nervous."

Hannah blushed as he spoke.

Luke continued. "I guess you dropped it near our table yesterday. I picked it up, but I didn't recognize it until I was already home. I just hoped you'd call so I could give it back."

"My brother gave this to me," Hannah said. "You know, I used to say I was a month younger than my brother so I could pretend sapphire was my birthstone."

"That's really cute. Are you twins, then?"

"Uh, yeah." Hannah led Luke to the couch and said, "Do you want anything to drink?"

Hannah was halfway to the kitchen before he could answer, so he shouted, "Rum and Coke would be great, if you have it."

Of course. She should have remembered. He was drinking those the night before, wasn't he? Hannah grabbed some spiced rum from her cabinet and made two rum and Cokes. She put a lime wedge on the side of each glass.

Hannah sat the drinks down and took a seat next to Luke on the couch. It was a little uncomfortable for her, but he looked relaxed, and she tried to mimic his nonchalant manner.

"What do you do for work?" She asked him. She tried to keep the conversation away from Hunter as best she could.

"I'm a sports analyst. Fantasy sports, mostly, but I still write for networks sometimes. It keeps me busy, but I'd bet it's nothing like being a doctor."

Hannah must have looked surprised, because Luke answered her next question before she could ask: "In case you forgot, we did see each other at the hospital the other day."

That's right, Hannah thought. She was still flustered and could hardly think straight.

"What were you there for?" she asked, then raised a hand to her face. "If that's not too private, I mean."

"Just a visit," Luke said.

It wasn't really any of Hannah's business, but why so vague? She found she wanted to know everything about him. She noticed he had inched closer to her on the couch. His thigh was touching hers, just like it had in the limo. She felt weak yet alive.

He turned to face her and put his hand on her cheek. As he leaned closer, an odd look flashed across his face. He retreated.

"I need to make a phone call," he said.

"What? Now?" Hannah sank into the couch in disappointment.

He got up from the couch and walked towards the hallway leading to the bedrooms as he pulled out his phone. Hannah reflexively put her fingers to her lips as if she were trying to feel what she had missed. She got up from the couch and started walking around the living room.

A minute later, Luke returned.

"Sorry. I have to go."

Just as Hannah was thinking how tired she was of Luke always leaving, he put his hand around Hannah's shoulder, leaned in towards her, and said, "Good night, Hannah." She could smell his cologne. Her frustrated thoughts were erased by an irresistible urge.

She leaned in closer and kissed him. His lips were soft and warm on hers. She moved her hand up to his neck and held onto him. She never wanted to stop kissing him. They continued to kiss until Hannah realized she hadn't been breathing. She pulled away and stared into his green eyes, thinking she could stay there for an eternity.

Luke gazed back, smiled at her, then gave her another quick kiss.

As he left, she watched him through the window. He turned back once before he got into his car and drove away.

It was then that she noticed: BMW, black, two doors. It was just as her brother had described in his journal, wasn't it? Hannah wanted to deny it, but there was only one way to tell for sure.

Hannah went straight to her room and pulled the journal out of her nightstand, turning to January 1st.

Chapter Eleven

There it was, just as Hannah remembered: a *black BMW coupe*. She flopped onto her bed as she considered this. It could have been just a coincidence, couldn't it? After all, it was just a car.

But small details resurfaced in her mind: his intense gaze when they first met, how well he seemed to know her already, and his odd behaviour—always disappearing before they could get too close. Did he have anything to do with those chocolates?

She scanned ahead to see if there was ever another mention of the car. Sure enough, on the second paragraph of the entry for February 9th, it made another appearance:

Anyway, I saw that black BMW again. It seemed to be waiting for me as I left work for the day. I kept my distance, but now I'm pretty sure I'm being watched. What does this asshole want? This is the last thing I need right now.

Hannah wished Hunter were there to explain everything. She reached for the ring below her neck. *I need him*, Hannah thought. She searched the journal for their birthday to find out what he had to say about the ring. It would be some comfort, at least.

But where she expected to find the entry for August 17th, there was nothing. In fact, the last few weeks of his life were missing—cut out cleanly near the spine. She thought about Luke disappearing down the hallway just minutes earlier. Is *that* what he had really been doing? And if it was, how had he known about the journal?

Hannah despaired. She should have dug for clues when she still had the chance. Those last few journal entries had been her shot of finding out what her brother was doing on the water that night.

Suddenly, Hannah had a desperate thought. She turned to the front of the journal: the calendar section. Hunter *had* used those pages, after all.

The square for August 26th read *Gala*, as expected, but it was crossed out. Below it and circled were three letters: HAC.

Hannah pried her laptop open and ran a search for the three letters. A dozen pages of results yielded nothing that seemed relevant. She tried to remember what she had read in Hunter's last entry. He had mentioned a cruise ship, hadn't he? Hannah tried another search, this time adding the word *cruise* to her search terms.

This time, she found something. Halfway down the third page was a business directory listing for a Heavy Anchors Co. in Victoria, BC. They had a phone number, an address, and a website.

That is, they once had a website. The link was dead. Hannah grabbed her phone to call the number listed. Their office was probably closed for the day, but at least she could leave a message.

Hannah had no luck with the phone number either. It was disconnected.

It was too much for her. Every time she seemed closer to learning more, the trail would end. She was frustrated, scared, and above all, mentally drained.

Hannah closed her laptop, put her phone on the charger, and climbed under the covers without brushing her teeth. She knew it would be hard for her to get any sleep, but she still had work in the morning.

CHAPTER TWELVE

Hannah's phone rang, startling her. She patted her hand along the bed beside her until she found it. She squinted at the bright light as she tried to see who was calling her, but she couldn't make out the words. She answered the call.

"Hello?" Hannah said.

"Hi, Hannah. This is Tracy from Heavy Anchors Co." The woman's voice sounded almost computerized. Hannah wondered if it was a real person or just a recording she was speaking to.

"I am calling to confirm your midnight cruise on August 26, 2017."

"I don't understand," Hannah replied, barely finding her voice.

"He's waiting for you. See you then!" The woman hung up before Hannah could say anything else.

Hannah pulled her phone away from her cheek and stared at the screen. Suddenly, the screen when black, and a second later, Hunter's face appeared on it. His lips and skin were a pale blue. She watched as a tear streamed down his cheek. He opened his mouth and spoke.

"I miss you, Hannah."

Hannah shot up in bed, out of breath. Her clothes were damp. She looked at her hands and saw that her phone wasn't there. It was sitting on the nightstand where she had left it when she went to bed.

Hannah rushed to the washroom and splashed cold water over her face. She stared at herself in the mirror trying to pull herself together. Her eyes were bloodshot, and the image of her brother's lifeless face flashed into her mind again. She lowered herself onto the edge of the bathtub until her heartbeat slowed down.

When she was once again strong enough to stand, Hannah returned to her bedroom and checked the time on her phone. Only minutes remained until her alarm would ring to wake her up for work. It didn't feel like she had gotten much sleep, but the time for that was over.

Before she left home, Hannah returned to her room to grab the journal. She wasn't letting it out of her sight anymore.

*   *   *

Hannah walked through the double doors into the main lobby of the hospital. The environment was comforting. It felt safe—and she needed the distraction.

She took the elevator to her department's staff lounge and used her access card to get in. She needed her doctor's coat, and she wanted to lock up the journal. But when she put her combination in and opened the locker, something unexpected was sitting there.

It was her ring, just where she would have left it before starting her shift. She brought her hand to her neck to see if the ring was still attached to her necklace. It was. Hannah couldn't understand. She picked up the other ring and held it close to her face. It was the same—the same sapphire stone with the same two diamonds surrounding it.

There was something else, though. On the shelf, underneath where the ring had been, was a note: *Stay away from the man with the green eyes.*

Hannah looked around the room to make sure she was alone. She sat on the couch and rubbed her forehead with her hands. *Have I lost my mind? Is this real? Or am I just dreaming again?* She didn't know how much more she could take. She didn't know who to trust.

Hannah went to the charge desk and had her manager paged. She knew that she wouldn't be able to focus on work after everything that had happened. She needed to figure this out.

In a few minutes, her manager arrived. "Good lord, Hannah! You look like hell. Are you sure you should be working overtime today? I think you could use some rest."

"That's what I called you here about," Hannah said. "I was feeling okay yesterday, but—"

"Say no more. I'll take you off the schedule for today and tomorrow—we'll be fine. Just give us a call before your shift on Wednesday, alright? And take care of yourself."

Hannah rushed out of the building and sat in her car for a few minutes. She knew she needed rest, but she didn't want to go home. Still, where else could she go?

Finally, she drove out of the parking lot. But when she reached her neighbourhood, she didn't turn down her street. Instead, she kept driving—towards the beach.

Hannah parked and found a quiet spot to sit on the warm sand. Her hair blew in the wind as she arranged her thoughts in order. As the breeze blew past her, she could almost swear she felt Hunter's presence. It was like he was trying to tell her something. As she stared out into the water, she recounted the strange events and discoveries from the past few days. She broke down each in her mind, looking for connections. She could only think of one.

She needed Hunter's courage. She grabbed her wallet out of her purse and pulled out a folded piece of paper. It was the article. She could never bring herself to throw it away.

She carefully straightened the folds and saw her brother's picture. He was smiling and happy. He didn't look like someone who should be dead. He was loving and kind and would have done anything for her. She read the headline: *Drowned Man Found at Local Beach.*

They said an anonymous tipper called in the body at around one in the morning. As far as they knew, Hunter was alone when he died. They said he must have slipped, hit his head, and fell into the water, drowning before he regained consciousness. There was no sign of a struggle besides the gash on his forehead—no sign that he fought against drowning. But he met with someone that night. Or, at least he meant to. Did that meeting ever happen? And if so, maybe his death hadn't been an accident after all.

Hannah pulled out her phone and scrolled through her contacts until she found the name she was looking for. She dialed his number and waited as it rang.

"Hey, Hannah."

She interrupted before he could say anything more. "Were you stalking my brother before he died?" The words ran together in a furious stream.

"What? No, of course I didn't—your brother died? I'm so sorry, Hannah. I didn't know."

"There was a black BMW following him. Was that or was that not you? Please be straight with me, Luke. I'm not in the mood for any bullshit."

Luke was silent for a moment. "Of course it wasn't me, Hannah. I didn't even know you had a brother until yesterday."

Hannah realized what she was doing and felt utterly embarrassed. If she wasn't crazy already, she definitely seemed like it now. She didn't know how to come back from this.

"I'm sorry. Forget I asked."

There was a longer pause this time. Hannah thought he might have hung up on her.

"Hannah, are you alright?" Luke asked, his voice warm and sincere.

When she didn't respond, he spoke again. "Where are you? I'm coming to see you."

She told him where she was and hung up the phone. Hannah knew now that she was going to have to tell him about her brother.

She didn't talk about it with anyone, even her best friend. She sat there waiting.

Staring.

Lost.

CHAPTER THIRTEEN

She heard his flip-flops as he came closer, but she didn't look back. She knew it was him. He sat beside her on the sand and put his hand on the small of her back. He pulled her in close, and she could smell his cologne again. It was intoxicating.

He didn't say anything. She was surprised—she had expected some sort of defence or reassurance. Instead, he just sat with her.

Finally, Hannah decided to speak. She felt comfortable with Luke. She wanted to trust him.

Her voice was quiet. "My twin brother died almost a year ago. He was my best friend."

Luke didn't say anything. He just waited. It was like he knew she just wanted him to listen. It was like he knew she would speak when she was ready.

"I miss everything about him. A few days ago, I received something from someone pretending to be my brother. At least, that's what I think they were doing. And then the stalker, then the ring, then the boat—I don't know what to think. I'm scared."

Luke grabbed her hand. He looked into her eyes and slowly brought his face to hers. She couldn't read his expression. He kissed her gently and then put his forehead on hers.

"Everything is going to be alright. You just need to tell me what's been happening. I want to help." His demeanour was calm but protective as he spoke.

When Hannah didn't respond, Luke stood up and brushed the sand from his pants. "Come with me," he said, reaching for her hand.

He led her to the parking lot where his car was parked, then he unlocked the car and opened the door for her.

"I'll drive you back later—unless you want to take your car home first."

"No," Hannah said, "that's okay. It should be fine here."

She didn't know where he was taking her, but she didn't care. She just wanted to be with him. She couldn't stand to be alone. His window was partly rolled down and her hair ruffled as they drove. When they stopped at a red light, he held her hand on the centre console and kissed it.

Hannah looked at him intently. "You're too good to be true. Sometimes I feel like you can't be real."

He didn't say anything back. He focused his eyes on the road ahead. Soon, he pulled into an upscale neighbourhood filled with picture-perfect houses. Hannah used to walk in neighbourhoods like this and dream about one day living in a big house overlooking the water. He turned into a cul-de-sac and pulled into the driveway of a beautiful two-storey home. The yard looked freshly landscaped. There was a front porch with beautiful patio furniture surrounded by fresh flowers. He got out of the car and went to her side to open her door. He led her to the front of the house, unlocked the door, and punched some numbers into a keypad inside.

Hannah lagged behind. She stood in the doorway and looked around the place from top to bottom. She was overwhelmed by how beautiful and tidy the house was. The décor looked straight out of a magazine, and there wasn't a hint of clutter.

She met him in the kitchen and sat at the island, almost afraid to smudge the shiny, stone countertop. Luke opened the fridge and grabbed two bottles of beer.

"You live here?" she said, still taking in her surroundings.

"I moved here just over a year ago. Used to rent a dingy apartment in downtown Vancouver, believe it or not."

Hannah *couldn't* believe it. Luke had incredible taste, and he took excellent care of the place. She had no idea you could make that kind of money writing about sports.

He led her up some stairs and opened a door. It led to a large balcony. Outside, there was comfortable-looking lounge furniture, plenty of plants, and a beautiful view of the ocean.

If I lived here, Hannah thought, *I would never leave.* She sat down and sunk into the cushions of the patio couch. Luke followed and sat next to her. He grabbed her hips and lifted her onto his lap.

"Tell me everything that's been happening to you. You can trust me," he said.

Hannah wanted to trust him. She wanted to so bad. She had never been so taken by someone, and she couldn't bear thinking that he had something to do with Hunter's death. *Well*, she thought, *if it was him, it couldn't hurt to tell him what he already knows.*

She started from the beginning—from when the oversized box of chocolates appeared on her doorstep. She told him about the card that was attached and how it was the same box that her brother would get for her. She surprised herself when she told him about her nightmares. She surprised *him* when she told him about the second ring. Hannah didn't mention the note or the journal, though. She wasn't ready to share those details yet.

Still, Hannah was surprised how easy it was to tell him all of this. She was relieved to finally be able to talk to someone. It had been feeling as though it were eating away at her insides to keep everything to herself.

There was a softness in his eyes as she unveiled her story—not mere pity, but genuine concern. When she finished, he gently rubbed her hair as they looked out in silence.

After some time, he looked back at her.

"It's going to be okay, Hannah. We'll figure this all out." His confidence was convincing.

They sat outside holding each other for a while, lost in their thoughts. Eventually, Luke spoke up.

"You don't work tomorrow, do you?"

Hannah shook her head.

"You shouldn't be alone tonight. You can stay here—in the spare bed, of course. I'll order us some food."

Hannah's remaining doubts about her safety around Luke were vanishing. She smiled and nodded. "I'd like that."

When the food arrived and Luke returned to the patio with the takeout boxes and another pair of beers, he also brought a soft, warm blanket and draped it over Hannah's shoulders. The sun was retreating, but a slight breeze still blew in from the water.

Hannah was getting more and more comfortable with Luke by her side. As they ate, they talked about their lives and dreams. Luke chuckled when Hannah admitted she eventually wanted a house like his.

They stayed out on the patio until after the sun had set. When the first stars began to appear, Hannah told Luke about her childhood and how she used to look at the stars every night. Luke shared his story about the time he went to space camp as a kid. Hannah was surprised—she hadn't pegged him as a space camp kind of guy.

She was falling for him hard.

Somewhere between the stars and his eyes, she fell asleep.

* * *

She was back at the beach. This time her feet were planted in the water, sinking slowly into the sand as the waves came in and out. It was so dark she couldn't make out her surroundings. It was then she noticed how cold she felt. Her teeth were chattering. She tried to walk, but her feet were buried deep, and more sand settled on top of them with each wave that passed. Soon, the water was waist-deep. Hannah tried to wriggle and fight her way out, but no matter how hard she tried, she couldn't move. She heard a noise behind her and quickly turned to see what it was.

In the darkness she saw a man. She squinted and came to realize it was Hunter. He was standing on the shore, still and silent. She started to scream his name. She screamed for him to help her as the water rose to her shoulders. He wouldn't move. She reached her arm towards him as the water covered her head.

Somehow, she heard a warning in his voice: "Stay away from the man with the green eyes."

Under the water, everything was black. It was like she was engulfed in thick mud. She was paralyzed and helpless. As she panicked, the last of the breath that she had been holding escaped. Just as she was about to inhale a lungful of water, she started shaking.

CHAPTER FOURTEEN

"Hannah. Hannah, it's okay. Wake up—it's just a dream." Luke was holding her shoulders and trying to calm her down.

She looked around, disoriented. Her dreams seemed to be getting more realistic. She was shivering and couldn't seem to warm up.

Luke wrapped her in a thick feather duvet and held her close to him. She hadn't realized it until he put the blanket on her, but she was in a bed. Daylight streamed in from beneath the window shade.

Hannah didn't even remember falling asleep. The last thing she remembered was being out on the balcony.

"I carried you upstairs after you drifted off last night," Luke explained before she could ask. "What were you dreaming about?"

"I drowned," Hannah said.

She couldn't help but hang on to the feeling of helplessness as her own brother watched her die. She knew it was a dream, but somehow it felt personal and real. What did it mean?

"Just relax. It'll be okay." Luke got up and left the room. He came back a couple of minutes later with a steaming mug of coffee. He brought the cup over to her and sat on the chair next to the bed.

Hannah became self-conscious as she thought about her appearance. She tried to comb her hair through with her fingers and rubbed under her eyes to make sure that her makeup hadn't smeared. She sipped on her hot coffee as he watched her.

"You can use my shower if you like," he said. "I'll take you back to your car in a bit. Just take your time for now."

"Thanks. That would be good. I almost forgot I left it at the beach." Hannah didn't feel like herself. She had been off ever since the moment she woke up.

Hannah was still feeling a little disconnected when Luke drove her to her car. He must have noticed something was wrong. He grabbed Hannah's cheek gently with his hand, pulled her in towards him and kissed her on the lips.

"I'll check on you later today, okay? If you need anything, call me."

"Yeah . . ." Hannah said. "Okay."

Hannah headed straight home from the beach. As soon as she had changed out of yesterday's clothes, she pulled Hunter's journal out of her purse and sat on the couch.

Before long, she found another mention of her brother's stalker.

February 23, 2017

I saw the man again. I went out to the pub for wings with my friends from school, and he was there. Watching. Who knows how long he was sitting there before I noticed him. At first, I noticed the sunglasses. Weird time and place to be wearing them. But what really set me off was that he didn't turn away from me the entire time. I couldn't help but feel like I knew that man. Something about him seemed so familiar. I decided to confront him, but when I got up and started walking towards him, I was bumped by a waitress carrying a tray of drinks. I turned to make sure I hadn't made her drop anything (I didn't), and when I looked up, he was gone. I only took my sights off of him for a moment, so I thought I might still catch him in the parking lot. No sign of him or his car.

I still don't know who he is, but I'm getting really sick of this.

Hannah tried to make a list of enemies Hunter might have had, but no one came to mind. Everyone loved her brother, and she couldn't think of anyone he had ever upset. Hunter would have done anything to avoid confrontation.

Hannah decided she needed to speak to her parents. She wanted to hear a comforting voice—even if the person speaking that voice wasn't so comforting anymore. She dialled their landline and waited as it rang. Her mother answered, as expected.

"Hi Mom, it's Hannah." She tried to sound put together, even though she knew her mother probably wouldn't notice.

"Oh, hello Hannah. How is everything in Victoria?"

"It's fine. I've been thinking of Hunter a lot lately."

"That's great! You know, I just got back from a hot yoga class. It's really quite something! You should come with me the next time you visit. You know Debbie from the book club? Well, her daughter . . ."

Just as Hannah expected. She wasn't going to get a *real* conversation out of her mother. Still, it was nice to hear her talk.

Hannah listened to her mother until she had run out of things to say. Finally, after about forty-five minutes, she went to make lunch and passed the phone to Hannah's father.

"Hey, Hannah. How are you?"

"Hi, Dad . . ." Hannah felt the urge to ask her father a question that had been on her mind since the other night. If anyone knew the answer, it would be her father.

"Have you ever heard of a cruise company called Heavy Anchors?"

The line was silent. Hannah quickly checked her phone to make sure her father hadn't hung up.

"Never heard of it," he finally said.

Hannah wasn't entirely convinced. Still, it wasn't unusual for her father to be distant and slow to respond. Hannah wondered if she was just being paranoid to doubt his answer.

"Look, Hannah, it's good to hear from you, but I've gotta go. Talk to you another time."

No, something was definitely odd about her father's behaviour. He was reserved, sure, but she knew he had nowhere to be. She had to get to the bottom of this. If her father wasn't going to help her, she would need to take matters into her own hands.

Unfortunately, all she had to go on was her brother's journal.

Chapter Fifteen

While it brought her some comfort, it made Hannah feel guilty to read her brother's words. It wasn't that she felt bad for intruding—that she thought he would disapprove. She knew Hunter would understand under the circumstances.

What bothered Hannah was that the things she read were all so new to her. She remembered the times Hunter would sit patiently and listen to her stories without a word about his own life. Hannah had no idea what had been going on with *him*. She hadn't bothered to ask.

Worse, Hannah still wished he were there to listen. She needed him. She wanted to hear him tell her that everything was going to be alright. She resented the book for not being able to provide that for her.

Nobody could give her what Hunter had given her when he was alive. Clearly, her parents were poor substitutes. Tawn was a good friend, but their most serious conversations had been about whatever minor sin her newest ex-boyfriend had committed against her. Luke . . . Luke made Hannah happy, but she still had lingering doubts about him.

Hannah resolved to put her feelings aside and try to focus on the mystery of her brother's death. She traded one set of frustrations for another. Who had been following her brother? What did they want from him? How did they convince him to cancel his evening plans and meet with them on the water? Did they ever meet? And if they did, what happened there?

Hannah hated not knowing the answers to her questions. As a doctor, she was used to having the answers—or at least she could find them when she needed to. Burn patients needed skin grafts. Cleft palates needed incisions and stitches. Patients had examinations and medical histories. Hannah was struggling with all the loose ends and gaps in the story. She couldn't put it together no matter how hard she tried.

Hannah went to the kitchen and grabbed a beer from the fridge. She noticed there were only a few left. Ignoring the obvious conclusion to that fact, she took her beer and the journal out on the patio.

One thread at a time, Hannah thought. Her guilt motivated her to choose the one least likely to hold the answers to her brother's death—but the one she regretted her ignorance about the most. Who was this Nicole?

Before long, Hannah found her name.

March 6, 2017

I met someone today. Her name is Nicole. She accidentally grabbed my drink at the coffee shop, and when I noticed, I grabbed hers and ran after her. She had the most beautiful smile. We didn't talk for long, but I asked for her number. Thank god she's single.

I texted her today (rookie move, I know) and we arranged to meet for dinner later this week. I don't know what it is, but I've got a really good feeling about her.

A few pages later, Hannah found mention of Nicole once again.

March 9, 2017

I had an amazing night. I took Nicole to my favourite restaurant (the Mexican one by the pier). She loved it. We talked all night about our lives, our upbringings, our families, and our plans for the future. I've never had a first date go so well.

When I dropped her off at home, she invited me to her friend's house for a party next weekend. I told her I would be her designated driver. Can't handle hangovers like I used to, and I'm working the next morning. Still, I just want to spend more time with her. She's all I can think about.

Well, almost. I still worry about the guy who's been following me, but I haven't seen any sign of him in a couple of weeks. Maybe I scared him off when I chased him from the pub. I'm glad, because I don't know how I'd handle it if he came around when I was with Nicole.

Hannah could see where this was going. Over five months he had been with her, and Hannah hadn't known a thing about it. As she brought her empty bottle back inside and grabbed a new one, she wondered if she had ever run into Nicole in town. She probably had, considering they went to the same coffee shop.

Hannah sat outside for a while, just trying to remember any signs that her brother had been in a relationship. She couldn't think of even one. Had Hunter been hiding it? Or had she just been that bad of a sister that she didn't notice?

She took the last few sips of her beer. The air was starting to cool as the sun lowered in the sky. She listened to the sound of the leaves fluttering in the breeze and could hear the ocean making its way in and out with the breath of the waves. She tried to calm her mind. She tried to stay in the moment in hopes that with a clear mind she would be able to uncover some part of the truth that she had been missing.

She read through several more days of the journal. There was more about Nicole, but nothing else seemed to stand out. For the most part, Hunter seemed happy with Nicole around, though there was the occasional day where he felt like the pressure was getting to him. He was still spending time with his friends. He was still going to work every day. Hannah was about to flip the page again when she saw someone out of the corner of her eye.

She didn't have to turn her head to know who was there. She put the journal down and tried to cover it with the pillow as she got up. She walked towards him, and when she got close enough he grabbed her waist and pulled her into him. They kissed with an intensity she had never experienced before.

Luke pulled his face back and looked into Hannah's eyes. He held the side of her face in his hand. She felt like he could see right through her soul.

"I'm taking you for dinner. You need to eat."

She knew he wasn't going to take no for an answer.

Chapter Sixteen

Luke took Hannah to an upscale Italian restaurant downtown. When they walked in, they were immediately directed to a private table at the back of the restaurant. The staff all seemed to know Luke.

"Do you come here a lot?" Hannah asked.

"I guess you could say that," he answered. "The owner and I play hockey together."

Hannah wasn't surprised by his answer. He seemed like the type to have connections in many unexpected places.

She sat across from him at the candlelit table. The lighting was dark in the restaurant, and it was a lot fancier than her usual dining spots. Hannah realized she was starving the second she saw a waiter carrying a plate to another table. She inhaled the smell of fresh pasta and it made her stomach growl.

Another waiter came soon after to take their drink orders. Luke wasted no time in ordering a bottle of sparkling wine.

Hannah started to protest. "I'm more of—"

"A lager drinker? I know. Don't worry. You'll like this."

Hannah was skeptical, but she loved how assertive he was. When the wine arrived, she found he was absolutely right as well. The wine was cold, crisp, and just slightly sweet. It was nothing like the syrupy stuff Tawn liked to drink.

She loved that he knew things she would like, despite the fact that they barely knew one another.

When Hannah picked up the menu and noticed the prices, she almost spilled wine on herself. Luke just chuckled. "Don't worry about it."

Soon, Hannah was comfortable. *Very* comfortable. Luke's charm had won her over entirely. They laughed and talked for hours. Luke told Hannah he had lived in Sweden when he was young, which she thought was fascinating. He didn't really fit her expectation of what someone from Sweden should look like. He was definitely tall, but he was missing the blonde hair and blue eyes she had pictured. He told her how he moved to Canada when he was seven and had lived in British Columbia ever since. He told her about his siblings, Matthew and Amara, and how they were still quite close and visited each other often.

Hannah was surprised that she wasn't put off by how much he talked about himself. It usually bothered her when the men she dated took control of the conversation. This time, she found it nice for some reason.

Eventually, most of the other customers had cleared out. Hannah hadn't even noticed the time passing. She realized how nice it was to have a distraction from everything, even if it was only for a few hours. She wanted so badly to trust Luke. She wanted to tell him about the journal. But still, something was holding her back.

Luke got up to talk to the waiter as she gathered her purse and got ready to leave. She had just finished looking at the time when her phone buzzed in her hand. She looked at the number and studied it. It wasn't a number she was familiar with. She opened up the text message, and all the muscles in her body tensed.

Did you enjoy the chocolates? You look beautiful tonight.

Hannah felt sick to her stomach. It was clear now that someone was definitely messing with her. She scanned her eyes across the restaurant to see if there was anyone watching her. Finally, she turned to Luke. He was holding his phone.

Luke swung around to face Hannah, and his smile faded.

"Are you alright?" he asked. "You look pale."

"I think I need to go home." Hannah felt desperate and helpless.

Luke grabbed her hand and she felt herself pull away. She was scared. She felt alone. The past year hadn't been kind to Hannah, and just as she almost felt like she could finally live her life without breaking down every day, she was knocked back to square one—or worse. She wished Hunter were there. She wished she could have helped him. Why couldn't he just have talked to her? Why hadn't he told her about the man? About the meeting? Hannah's thoughts were a mess. Before she knew it, she was out in the parking lot ordering an Uber.

Luke hadn't left her side. He could see what she was doing.

"Hannah, what's going on? One minute you were fine, and now . . . If something's wrong, let me help you." His voice was genuine. But Hannah had to be sure.

"Let me see your phone," Hannah demanded.

Luke didn't hesitate for a second. He passed the phone to her, holding his thumb on the fingerprint sensor.

She went into his messages. The most recent text was between Luke and his friend Mark. Hannah was a few names down. *Great, see you then.* Nothing about the chocolates.

Luke just watched as Hannah proceeded to check his recently opened apps. Sports, email, Facebook—nothing suspicious. It wasn't Luke after all.

Hannah felt relieved until she remembered that if it wasn't him, it was someone else. Someone who could be watching her at that very moment.

She decided to show Luke. She passed his phone back and then showed him the text on her own. As Luke read the message, his eyes narrowed, and his face started turning red.

"Let's go, Hannah. I'll take you home."

He led her to his car and opened the door for her. When he got in, he was silent for a minute or two. Hannah felt terrible for doubting him.

Hannah leaned over the middle armrest and put her head on Luke's lap. "I'm so sorry, Luke. I didn't want to think it was you, I just . . ."

Hannah could feel Luke's muscles soften.

"Don't be sorry. I'm not upset. Not at you." Luke stroked Hannah's shoulder for a few minutes, then said, "Are you sure you want to go home? You can stay at my place again. You don't need to be on your own."

"Yeah, I'll be fine. I have work tomorrow anyway."

"If you're sure. If you change your mind, you know where I am."

Luke started the engine and began to pull out of the parking lot. Hannah kept her head where it was. She was comfortable. The engine purred as Luke smoothly took them down the road.

Suddenly, Luke slammed on the brakes. Hannah felt dazed—then, pain.

"Jesus! What the hell—Hannah, are you alright?"

Hannah reached to her head where it had hit the steering wheel. Her rib hurt from the gear stick, and her knee had rammed into the glove box.

"I think so . . . What happened?"

"Some psycho just ran a red in front of us. Black car. Didn't get the . . . Wait, do you think—"

"Follow him." Hannah sat up, ignoring the pain, and buckled her seatbelt. Luke whipped the car down the street the other car took.

They followed the road for a few minutes, but the car that ran in front of them was nowhere to be seen. Finally, they gave up, and Luke turned back towards Hannah's neighbourhood.

When they arrived, Luke put his hand on Hannah's leg. "It's not too late to change your mind, Hannah. You can stay with me. I'll drive you to work in the morning."

"No, really, it's fine. Thanks, Luke, but I just . . . I'll be okay. I'll text you before I go to sleep and when I get up in the morning."

Luke sighed and then nodded. "Alright. You know where I live." He paused, and his expression hardened. "We're going to find out who this person is, Hannah."

He kissed her goodnight.

*　*　*

Luke watched Hannah walk up the steps and into her house. Once she was safe inside, he scanned the neighbourhood. He sat there for twenty minutes before he was satisfied, finally shifting into gear and heading home. Before it was out of sight, he took one last look at Hannah's house in the rear-view mirror.

PART TWO

Chapter Seventeen

Almost a year had passed since Luke's late-night visit to the beach. Eleven months and twenty-two days, to be exact. There wasn't a day that went by without it crossing his mind. The memory stayed with him like a shadow.

He had stayed away from this particular beach ever since—but on this day, Luke was drawn to it. It was because of James, his friend and business partner; after crashing his car the night before, James was in the hospital. He was lucky. Minor injuries.

But the thought that James could have died brought Luke back to the beach. He remembered the body he found there. That body was once a man with a life and a family—and friends. Who was missing that man? How had their lives irreversibly changed?

Luke worked through his thoughts as he sat on the stone steps near the water. If it wasn't for James, Luke wouldn't have been in Victoria at all. It was he who suggested they take their little hockey pool and grow it into a public fantasy sports service. Who handled the hosting, marketing, and sponsorships. Who helped Luke find a place when he finally agreed to move closer to James to focus on managing their runaway success.

But that man—what impact could he have had if he lived?

Luke couldn't help but think of the *other* man he saw that night.

The shadowy figure was etched into his memories. He wished he had had the courage to confront him instead of run. At the very least, he wished he had the courage to file a proper police report. How could some lone guy have spooked him so much?

He didn't know what the police eventually decided about the case, but the paper mentioned nothing about the other man. All they said was a man named Hunter Melbrook drowned and was found dead on the beach. But Luke knew there was more to the story.

Luke decided that was enough brooding for now. He had a friend to visit in the hospital.

Chapter Eighteen

Luke entered the hospital cradling a pair of coffees. He asked the receptionist where he could find his friend, and she directed him towards the elevators.

At that moment, he saw a doctor walking into an opening elevator. He sped towards it, hoping to catch it before the doors closed. But when she turned to face the lobby, he froze.

Something about her seemed so familiar. Luke tried to divert his gaze, but he couldn't will himself to move. He was lost in her eyes. Somehow, he recognized them. The elevator doors slowly closed as he stood there, stunned.

Just like that, she was gone. He hoped he'd be lucky enough to see her again.

When Luke got to his friend's room, James was glued to his phone. *Never stops working, that guy.* Luke put the spare coffee on the side table and cleared his throat.

James finally looked up. "Hey, buddy! I was wondering when you'd show up."

"Hey, James. How you feeling?"

"Oh, I'm fine. Car insurance is going to be a nightmare for a while, but it could have been worse. Speaking of which, this whole thing got me thinking. We should probably have life insurance policies out for each other, don't you think?"

Luke responded with a tight frown.

"Lighten up, buddy! Just saying."

Luke changed the subject. "So what's the damage?"

"Total write-off. It's okay, though. I was getting tired of the—"

"Your leg, James."

"Right. Well, they still want to do some x-rays, but they say it's probably just a few torn ligaments. I'll be out of the league for a few weeks at least."

Luke's expression lightened. "Damn shame. We might actually win a game or two without you."

"Hah! There's the Luke I know."

Luke took a sip of his coffee and sat on the chair next to the bed. "So do you need me to get anything from the office for you?"

"Nah. I should be out of here by the afternoon. I can get everything done on this for now," James said, waving his phone. "You could do *something* for me, though."

Luke cocked his head. "What's that?"

"This evening. Bar. Drinks. You're buying."

"I don't know, do you really think you should—"

"Come on, Luke. Are you going to make a cripple beg?"

Luke smirked. "I thought you said you were fine."

James dropped his forehead and gave Luke a pleading look. "Alright, I'll go."

"Damn right you will!"

*　*　*

Luke left James's room feeling a little lighter. His friend had a knack for cheering him up. Luke felt his mind drifting back to the body on the beach, but he resisted the thought.

When he reached the elevators, Luke remembered the woman he had seen in the lobby and cursed himself for not checking her ID badge for her name. He kept an eye out for her the rest of the way out of the hospital.

CHAPTER NINETEEN

Luke took a cab to the bar and arrived with time to spare. There were no free tables, so he pulled up to a bar stool and ordered himself a rum and Coke. While he waited, he glanced idly around the bar.

When he saw her, he couldn't believe his eyes. There she sat at a crowded table with birthday balloons and gifts. He kept his eye on her for a long time. At one moment, a newcomer approached, gave her an enthusiastic hug, and shouted, "Happy birthday, Hannah!" over her shoulder.

Hannah. He needed to know her. There was something about her that drew him in. He didn't know what it was yet, but he had a feeling he would soon find out. Luke watched intently and waited for an opportunity to approach to her.

Soon after, he saw her finish her beer and get up to go to the restroom. He knew this was his chance to make an impression. He ordered a couple of shots and turned to face the hallway, hoping she would recognize him when she returned.

She saw him immediately once she turned the corner again. She stood there, almost frozen, and that's when he knew she felt it too. He signalled her over and patted the seat next to him. He wanted to be close to her.

He couldn't quite find the words, so he slid over a shot. Finally, he managed to wish her a happy birthday.

"How did you know it was my birthday?" she said.

"I'm stalking you." It sounded funnier in Luke's head than it did out loud, and Hannah's expression agreed. "Bad joke? Sorry. I overheard some people wishing you happy birthday when you came in." Thankfully, she relaxed and started fiddling with a ring on her right hand. *Not married*, Luke thought. *That's a good sign.*

He took his shot and raised the empty glass. Hannah followed.

Luke smiled at the face she made as she lowered her glass.

He felt his pocket vibrate. *That must be James*, he thought. He pulled his phone out and read the screen. James needed help up the stairs. "Sorry. Gotta go."

Luke grabbed his wallet and started towards the door. Then, he stopped and turned back for a moment. "See you, Hannah."

Luke found James leaning on the handrail at the bottom of the stairs.

"This place really needs a wheelchair ramp," said James.

"That's funny. We've been here dozens of times, and I've never heard you say that before."

"Can it and take my crutches, will you?"

Luke grabbed them and put James's arm around his shoulder.

Back inside the bar, Luke scanned again for open tables. Luckily, there was one just becoming available. Unluckily, it was out of sight of Hannah's table. It was the best he could expect on a Friday night.

The two of them took their seats and ordered drinks. James was in high spirits and kept the conversation alive for a couple of hours. When it finally seemed to be running out of steam, James got a mischievous look on his face.

"You know what we should do?"

"What?"

"We should find you a girl. With me in crutches, I'd make the perfect wingman. We can come up with some story about how you saved my life. They'd be all over it!"

Luke shook his head. "You know I'm not into pickup games." He paused for a few moments. "Besides, I met someone before you showed up."

"Are you kidding? You got a girl's number in, what, twenty minutes?"

Luke slapped the table. "Damn it! I completely forgot to ask for it."

"Well, go look for her! Don't let me hold you back. I need to take a leak anyway." James ushered Luke off and reached for his crutches.

Luke cut a straight path to the birthday table. Several people were still there, but Hannah was nowhere in sight.

Luke raised his voice to be heard over the noise of the bar. "Sorry, but are you Hannah's friends?"

A girl with flashy designer clothing turned to look at him. "Oh! You're that guy she was talking to! You have *really* nice eyes." She obviously had more than a few drinks.

"Uh, thanks. Is Hannah still here?"

"Nope. She left forever ago. You can join us if you like, though."

"I should be getting back to my friend . . . but thanks anyway."

"Wait." She grabbed his arm. "We're going clubbing tomorrow night. You should come!"

Luke considered this. "Will Hannah be there?"

The girl looked a little disappointed, but she said, "I'll see what I can do." She unlocked her phone and handed it to him. "Give me your number and I'll text you the details."

Luke obeyed, smiling. He'd have another chance after all.

CHAPTER TWENTY

Luke went to sleep that night with thoughts of Hannah.

He awoke to a cold, wet feeling on the side of his face.

Luke jolted upright when he saw the dark, red blotch on his pillow. Blood. He rubbed his face, pulling his hand away to examine his sticky fingers. He felt no pain, but confusion and worry sent him to the bathroom mirror.

In his reflection, Luke studied the smudged patch of blood on his cheek. His ear was clean and, except for a tiny smear on the side, so was his nose. He lowered his face to the sink and scrubbed. The redness came away cleanly, leaving no sign of its source. *What the hell happened?* he thought. No reasonable explanation for spontaneous, untraceable bleeding came to mind.

Luke put the pillow case in the wash. The pillow itself he wrapped in a garbage bag and threw in the black bin in his garage. It couldn't be saved.

Put off—but unwilling to lose his mind on an isolated mystery—Luke decided to shower and get on with his day.

As he stepped out of the shower, Luke got a second message. The thick, reflective letters stood out on the foggy bathroom mirror. He stood transfixed, staring at the words.

Stay away from Hannah.

Suddenly, the splotch of red on his pillow had new meaning. Luke rushed to get dressed, pulled the bagged pillow out of the garbage bin, and practically ran to his car.

* * *

"What do you mean it's not real?"

"It's stage blood. Look." The officer rubbed the red spot on Luke's pillow then presented his finger. "It's still wet and perfectly red. Real blood dries brown." He gave Luke a reproaching look. "You think you're the first person to try this prank?"

"It's not a . . ." Luke gathered himself. "Look, whether it's real or not, someone broke into my house last night."

The officer's composure changed, but only slightly. "Did you find anything missing?"

"No. Well, I haven't checked. But there was a message on my bathroom mirror. A threat."

"Any sign of forced entry?"

Luke thought for a moment about his security system. It hadn't been armed when he left for the police station, and he normally set it before he went to bed. But he *had* been drinking the night before. Maybe he just forgot.

"No," Luke said. "Not that I've noticed."

The officer finally scribbled a brief note and closed his notebook. "I'll get you a form. If it makes you feel safer, we can send a car over to check it out later."

Luke left the police office without filing his complaint. If the other officers were as dismissive and unprofessional as the one he had just met, they wouldn't be any help. Besides, he had plans that evening. He wasn't going to let a little prank ruin his chances with Hannah.

Chapter Twenty-One

That afternoon, Luke got a text from Tawn, Hannah's friend, with the address to where.the group was meeting. He was relieved she remembered. The thought of seeing Hannah again practically erased the bad morning he had had. She stayed in his mind for the rest of the day.

When the evening came, Luke changed his clothes, styled his hair, and sprayed on a little cologne. With twenty minutes to spare, he had a rum and Coke before calling a cab.

Tawn answered the door when he rang. She didn't hide her excitement one bit. "Come in!" she said.

Luke followed her, keeping his eyes peeled for Hannah.

Tawn led him into the kitchen and introduced him to the others. Adrianna, the owner of the house, offered Luke a beer. He eased himself into the conversation as he sipped his beer. Still, every time he heard someone open the front door, he lost his place.

Soon, someone Luke recognized from the night before came in from the backyard. "Hey! You came after all!" The man bowled over to Luke and offered his hand.

Luke accepted the handshake. "Yeah, I guess I did. Luke. And you are . . ."

"Adam. Good to see you again, man." He spoke louder than he

needed to in the closed kitchen.

"You too," Luke answered.

Adam put his arm around Luke's shoulder and turned them both to face the patio door. "Hey, man." He lowered his voice. "I know you're here to see Hannah. That's cool. But there's something I should tell you."

"Look who's here!" Tawn interrupted from the hallway. Luke and Adam both turned, and Adam removed his arm from Luke's shoulder.

Hannah. Luke had almost missed her entrance. He kept his eyes trained on her as she greeted her friends, her eyes similarly glued to him. Clearly, she wasn't expecting him to be there. He smiled at her and could see her entire body tense.

Adam stepped back and put his hands in his pockets. He reintroduced the two of them.

"Yes, we met last night. Sorry, I forgot to ask your name," she said, her eyes now swimming in his. Luke noticed she was fidgeting—playing with her ring like she had the night before. He thought it was cute.

"Well, now you know—and I hope you won't forget," he replied.

Adrianna offered Hannah a glass of champagne. She barely responded, keeping her attention focused on Luke.

Minutes later, they were sitting at a table on the deck out back. Luke wanted to spend some time talking with Hannah, but the other guys on the deck fought for his attention. One asked Luke's opinion of an off-season hockey trade that had them all arguing. He answered honestly and completely, turning to Hannah to make sure she knew he hadn't forgotten her.

Unfortunately, the guys were impressed by his answer. Soon, they were having him settle other sports arguments and asking for advice on bets. He smiled and shrugged to Hannah. It seemed they were intent on preventing him from having a moment alone with her.

After almost a half hour of playing the sports guru, Luke saw his chance to cut out from the conversation when a few of his apprentices retreated inside with empty bottles. It proved unnecessary: Adrianna came outside at that moment to tell everyone the limo had arrived. Everyone made their way inside.

Luke wanted to make a gesture of apology to Hannah. He had noticed she was a beer drinker the night before, so he stopped in the kitchen to grab them a couple for the limo. *I'm sure the owner of these won't mind.*

* * *

As everyone piled out of the limo, Luke felt his phone vibrate. He reached into his pocket and clicked the side button to ignore the call. *If it's important*, he thought, *they'll leave a message.* He moved into the club, sticking to Hannah as best he could. Then, his phone gave another short buzz—apparently it *was* important.

Luke pulled his phone from his pocket and breathed a sigh of relief when he saw who the message was from: just his neighbour. Couldn't be anything major. He slipped his phone back and headed towards the bar with Hannah and Adam.

The bartender served Hannah first, and Adam practically jumped at the opportunity to pay for her drink. Luke felt a hint of jealousy. He hoped Adam was merely acting as a friend.

The three of them sat at a table near the bar, and Luke's spirit rose when Hannah shifted her seat nearer to his. Finally, a chance to get to know her. He practically ignored Adam. Still, the loud music made it difficult to exchange words. Luke and Hannah half-shouted to each other, repeating themselves and replacing words with gestures often. Luke's phone buzzed once again and, like before, he ignored it.

When they were only halfway through their drinks, Adam got their attention. He waved his empty bottle and shouted, "I'll get us another." Before Luke could decline, he was gone.

He turned to Hannah. It seemed like a good time to ask. He kept it as casual as the necessary volume allowed. "What's the deal between you and Adam?"

"Oh, it's nothing. We're just friends." She fidgeted for a moment, then started to stand. "I'll be right back."

Luke watched her walk away. He kept following her with his eyes until she turned down the hallway to the bathrooms.

He sat thinking for a moment. Then, he remembered his phone. He pulled it out and checked the notifications: two calls and two voice messages from his neighbour. Luke hit play on the first message and put his hand over his other ear as he raised the phone to his head.

"Hey, Luke. It's Dean. Your car alarm has been going off for an hour now, and I'm trying—"

Luke lowered his phone and skipped to the second message.

"Luke, answer your damn phone! If you don't get over here and shut that thing off, I'm going to pry the hood open and unplug the battery." The message ended.

Luke lowered his phone and threw his head back. He couldn't believe his luck. Just that moment, Adam was returning with drinks. "Hey," he shouted. "Something wrong?"

Luke got up. "Something came up. Have to leave." He moved closer to Adam and spoke right in his ear. "If I give you my number, can you make sure Hannah gets it?"

Adam smiled. "I can do better." He walked around the table and reached into Hannah's purse. He returned to Luke with her phone. "I know the code."

Luke was too intent on leaving his number to question this. He waited for Adam to unlock the phone, open the contact list, and hand it over. "Thanks."

"Any time." Adam waited for Luke to finish then returned the phone to Hannah's purse. "See you next time."

"Yeah. See you." Luke had begun to walk away when he felt

something under his shoe. He lifted his foot and saw something reflective. Crouching down, he examined it. It was a ring.

Without thinking much about it, Luke pocketed the ring and hurried out of the club.

CHAPTER TWENTY-TWO

Luke hurried out of the club and called a cab. Luckily, there was already a driver nearby. It was only minutes before he was in the back seat and on the way home.

He pulled up his call history and returned his neighbour's call. Dean picked up after one ring.

"Christ, Luke, I was one minute away from calling the cops. You got my message?"

Luke could hear the sound of his car alarm in the background. "Sorry, Dean. I mean it. I'll make it up to you for not breaking out the crowbar."

"You're on your way?"

"Yeah, I'll be there in under ten minutes. I'm in a cab now."

"Thank God. I should have been asleep an hour ago."

"Sorry," Luke said again.

After Dean told Luke about his early tee time and Luke apologized once more, they ended the call. Luke spent the rest of the drive hoping his car wasn't burglarized or backed into.

When the cab reached Luke's neighbourhood and approached his cul-de-sac, the noise became distinguishable. The driver cringed as he turned down Luke's street.

"That you, my friend?" he said, gesturing to the flashing lights of Luke's noisy BMW.

"Yep. That's me."

Luke paid and got out of the cab. Dean emerged from his house in a robe and slippers. He waved a baseball bat and grinned.

"Sorry!" Luke shouted. He glanced at his car. No damage that he could see. "Keys are inside! Just a second!"

Luke ran in, grabbed his key fob from the rack, and mashed the unlock button as he headed back outside.

"Next time," Dean said, waving the baseball bat again.

Luke nodded sheepishly and began inspecting his car. There was something underneath his wiper blade.

Dean noticed. "Got a ticket, eh? Serves you right." Looking satisfied with himself, he went back inside.

Luke lifted the wiper blade and grabbed what it had been holding down. It was a lined, notebook-sized sheet of paper. He unfolded it and found a message in big black letters.

Stay away from Hannah.

CHAPTER TWENTY-THREE

Luke couldn't remember getting any sleep that night. He tossed and turned, alternating between his stormy thoughts and desperate attempts to fall sleep. He thought about the fake blood and the threatening messages. Why did this person want to keep him from Hannah? And who would go to such lengths?

He dragged himself through the morning in a daze. Luke had some article deadlines coming up, but he just couldn't get the words out. After trying unsuccessfully for hours, he closed his computer.

Instead, Luke wandered the house, tidying aimlessly. When he reached his bedroom, he noticed the ring on his nightstand—the one he had pocketed the night before. He knew that ring. Memories of the past two nights streamed back to him. He recalled her adorable nervous habit of toying with it.

It was as good a sign as he could hope for. Luke didn't care who it was who left those threats. He was going to see Hannah again. If he had to, he would visit the hospital every day until he found her.

The ring was one thing, but Luke wanted to make a grander gesture. He checked his phone for the time. It was early afternoon on a Sunday. The mall would still be open for a few hours. He grabbed his keys and went straight out the door.

At the mall, Luke found an open jewellery store. He had decided what he wanted to get her on the way over. Hannah probably couldn't wear rings at work since she was a doctor, but she could wear a necklace. With a chain, she could wear her ring all the time—and wear Luke's gift as well.

Luke returned home all worked up. This time, it was excitement rather than anxiety. Hungry and in need of something to settle him down, he decided to make pasta and watch some baseball.

When he finished cooking, he took his plate and sunk into the couch. He noticed a light in his peripheral vision and turned to see his phone going off on the coffee table next to him. It was a text message from an unknown number. Luke's stomach turned as his fear of the intruder resurfaced. Did they know his number as well? Did they also know he had Hannah's ring?

He opened the message.

Did I scare you away yesterday?

Luke's unease held him in its grip. Why would they say that? Had they tried to catch him at home the night before?

He felt a surge of relief as he realized who the message was really from. Of course she would wonder why he left early. His relief doubled at the thought that it hadn't put her off entirely. Luke took his time finishing his food as he let his nerves settle.

He and Hannah traded a few messages back and forth. Before long, Luke asked her if he could go over and see her. He knew it was a bold thing to do, but it was a better chance to give her the gift than running into her at work.

Hannah agreed, and Luke grinned to himself. He had a couple of hours to spare before the agreed time, so he sat back and watched the rest of the game.

* * *

Luke pulled up to Hannah's house and grabbed the gift bag he'd prepared from his passenger seat. As he stepped out of his car, he looked around to check out the neighbourhood. He saw someone walking down the street. He couldn't make out a face, but the figure was wearing all black with a hat and sunglasses. *Sunglasses?* Luke thought. *In this light?* The broad-shouldered figure definitely belonged to a man. When the man saw Luke staring at him, he stopped walking and just stood there, staring back. Luke shivered.

He broke the standoff and headed to Hannah's door.

When Hannah appeared at the doorway, Luke forgot all about what he had just seen. Her beauty consumed his thoughts. He leaned against the doorframe and flirted a little, hiding the small gift bag. Soon, he was in her home.

Luke hadn't hesitated for a moment when he picked out the gift, but now he was getting a little self-conscious. Was a silver chain too forward when they had only spoken twice? He considered excusing himself and putting it back in his car, simply returning the ring instead. *No*, he thought, *it's too late now.* He gathered his courage and presented the bag.

"Here," he said.

Luke watched her unwrap it, hoping she would like it.

Hannah gasped. It seemed like joy on her face, but Luke couldn't tell for sure. He signalled for her to turn around, taking a few seconds to hide his worry as he put it around her neck. He could have sworn he felt goosebumps on her skin where he touched her.

He told her how he found the ring the night before and later recognized it as hers. Hannah blushed. The ring was apparently a gift from her twin brother. When she hinted that sapphires were her favourite gemstone, Luke made a mental note.

Hannah left Luke in the living room to pour them each a drink. When she returned, Luke was a little surprised to find his nerves gone. She seemed to like his gift, and conversation was easy. He couldn't help but move closer to her. He could smell her perfume and it made him crazy.

He had to kiss her.

He gently grabbed her cheek and moved her towards him. Hannah leaned in, looking directly in his eyes.

Something stopped Luke. When he looked in her eyes, he inexplicably remembered the man who had died on the beach. Luke suddenly felt a bit sick to his stomach. *Why now?*

He backed away and made up an excuse about having to make a phone call. Not the best cover, he admitted to himself, but he needed to clear his head. He walked down the hallway and pretended to make a call.

It didn't work. He couldn't get the image of that man out of his mind. Luke couldn't stay.

Frustrated and unsettled, he returned and told Hannah he had to go. The disappointment on her face killed him. He had to say something to salvage her feelings, but he didn't know what.

Instead, Luke put his hand around Hannah's shoulder, leaned in, and said, "Good night, Hannah."

Hannah did the rest. She kissed Luke intensely, and just for a moment he forgot about everything else.

Then, Luke left.

CHAPTER TWENTY-FOUR

Late that night, Luke shot up out of bed. He had water all over him, and his sheets were wet. It was pouring rain outside, and he hadn't closed the window. He was freezing cold. He got up out of bed, took the blankets and sheets off, and threw them into his laundry hamper in the closet. He then went to get some extra blankets from the linen closet down the hallway.

Luke stopped dead in his tracks when he felt the water under his feet. In the doorway of his room were footprints. He rushed down the stairs without even thinking. It was as though his legs were in control even if his mind couldn't keep up.

When he got downstairs, the house was dark. The large glass windows were covered in rain and he couldn't help but feel vulnerable. Whoever was just in his house could easily be watching him from outside.

Luke checked his security system and found it disarmed. Had he simply forgotten to arm it again, as he thought he must have two nights before? That didn't seem likely. Luke wasn't that forgetful.

Again, nothing seemed to be missing. Luke searched for messages, checking in all the likely places—even turning on the shower to steam up the bathroom mirror. Nothing. What else could he do?

Luke remembered his visit to the police station and doubted they would do anything for him. There was no evidence that his house had been broken into except for the wet footprints, and they wouldn't be very convincing.

Still, whoever was in his home wanted something. Luke just had no idea what that something was.

*   *   *

Luke's mind was once again consumed by the intruder. He hadn't slept any more that night, so when morning came, he went to the office early for a change of scenery. Work was the best distraction he had, and the kind of work he did for the fantasy sports site was exactly the kind he needed.

By late morning, Luke had already finished the day's work. He rolled his chair away from his keyboard and thought about Hannah. He wanted to send her a message, but he still couldn't quite think straight. Instead, he just remembered their kiss.

Luke was just about to give his articles another shot when his phone went off. It was Hannah. He fought off the urge to answer immediately and waited for two rings.

"Hey, Hannah," he said.

"Were you stalking my brother before he died?" Her tone was insistent. He almost didn't recognize her voice.

He wasn't sure what to make of that. Hannah pressed him, but he had no idea what she was talking about. He reminded her that he hadn't even known she had a brother until she said so. She apologized. An awkward silence followed.

Luke asked her if she was okay, but she didn't answer.

"Where are you?" he said. "I'm coming to see you." He needed to talk to her. He needed to know where all this was coming from.

When she told him where she was, he said he was on his way. But after he hung up, he paused. She was at the beach.

That beach.

CHAPTER TWENTY-FIVE

When Luke arrived at the beach, he quickly changed out of his dress shoes and into a pair of sandals he had in the back of his car. He made his way down the concrete steps and found Hannah sitting on the beach. He sat next to her and couldn't help but touch the small of her back.

After several minutes, Hannah finally spoke.

"My twin brother died almost a year ago. He was my best friend." Hannah's voice was quiet, but he caught every word.

Luke silently processed this. He wanted to ask her if her brother was found on that beach. He wanted to ask for her brother's name. He wanted to confirm his suspicions.

But Luke was afraid. He worried it might hurt things between them if what he suspected was true. He worried what she'd say about him being the one who discovered her dead brother—or what it would be like to keep it a secret if he decided to keep it from her.

He wasn't sure he really wanted to know the truth.

Instead, Luke waited for Hannah to speak. She told him that someone was impersonating her brother. Then, she started to break down. Luke's emotions shifted into anger at the thought of someone messing with the girl he was falling for.

He could see the loss in her eyes and couldn't begin to comprehend how she was feeling. Luke grabbed Hannah's hand, brought his face close to hers, and kissed her. He knew she needed someone to reassure her that everything would be alright, and so he reassured her. He kept his own thoughts and worries to himself.

I need to get her away from here, Luke thought. But the truth was, it was he who needed to get away.

Luke led Hannah back to his car, and she didn't protest when he suggested that she leave hers behind. Soon, they were pulling into Luke's driveway. He watched Hannah's expression as he led her into his home. She seemed hesitant. Luke grabbed of couple of beers from the fridge, hoping a light buzz would help her feel at ease.

"You live here?" she asked.

Luke felt relieved. She was merely impressed with his home, not frightened or intimidated.

He led her upstairs to the balcony. The weather was perfect, unlike the night before. Hardly a cloud in the sky. They sat on the patio couch, and Luke asked her to tell him everything that had been happening to her. He comforted her, sure that there was a reasonable explanation for it all.

That is, until she told him about a second ring. The same ring he had found and returned to her—there was a copy of it sitting in Hannah's locker at the hospital. Hannah insisted there had only been one.

Luke wondered if she might be losing her mind, but he quickly dismissed the thought. No, something really was going on. He wondered if the person who had been bothering her was the same one who had been threatening him to stay away from her. He remembered the shady man he saw on her street the night before. Was it him behind all of this? Or was Luke merely being paranoid?

Luke didn't want to take any chances.

"You shouldn't be alone tonight," he said. "You can stay here— in the spare bed, of course. I'll order us some food."

Hannah's reaction was grateful and affectionate. She squeezed him and said, "I'd like that."

They spent the rest of the afternoon on the balcony, easing into casual conversation. Hannah's apprehension seemed to have disappeared. Later, Luke wrapped her in a blanket and they ate together, still chatting comfortably about everything and nothing. *I might be in love with this woman*, Luke thought.

After a while, he could tell that Hannah was tired. Luke let her fall asleep on the couch and sat with his thoughts for a while as she slept. He stroked Hannah's hair gently as he played out what she told him over and over in his mind. Someone, he decided, wanted Hannah for themselves. Someone who wasn't above using mind games and intimidation.

I'll let someone or something come between me and Hannah over my dead body.

CHAPTER TWENTY-SIX

Once the sky was completely dark, Luke carried Hannah inside. She stirred a little but didn't wake.

Luke was tempted to carry Hannah to his own bed. He didn't think she would disapprove. Still, he had promised they'd sleep in separate beds, and he wanted her to trust him.

The next morning, Luke checked on Hannah on his way down to the kitchen to make coffee. She was still asleep, but the duvet was tossed aside. She twitched and breathed rapidly.

Luke shook her awake. "Hannah, it's okay. Wake up—it's just a dream."

When he asked her what she had been dreaming about, she said, "I drowned." Luke's stomach dropped. Whenever he heard the word *drown*, he always felt sick. He had to leave the room and decided to bring her some coffee.

He took some deep breaths when he waited for the machine to heat up. He knew that at some point he would come clean about what he had found on the beach almost a year before. He would have to tell her that someone had been threatening him to stay away from her. He was almost certain that their stories were connected, and they needed to work together to line them up. But Luke was scared to tell her. He was afraid she would push him away. Most of all, he was afraid of the truth. What if her brother *had* been murdered and Luke hadn't done anything to bring the killer to justice?

Luke pushed his thoughts aside and brought the coffee up to Hannah. He sat next to the bed and watched her take the first sip. Even with dishevelled hair and a poor night's sleep, she looked beautiful in the sunlight from the window. Luke decided he would do anything for her.

But for certain things, he needed time.

After a leisurely morning, Luke drove Hannah back to the beach to retrieve her car. He didn't want to leave her, but he had afternoon plans with his hockey buddies. They were all business owners and self-employed professionals, so they were able to take advantage of the easy weekday access to ice time. Still, it was hard to get them all together at once.

Before driving away, Luke promised he would check on Hannah that evening. He assured himself that she would be fine on her own until then.

Luke was glad to let off some steam at the rink. Sweat was pouring off him by the time their arena reservation was up. It felt good to be exhausted from having fun rather than from worry and restless nights. His friends commended him on his hustle and offered some post-game beers.

Luke showered in the change room and went to his locker to grab his clothes. When he got there, something wasn't right. His locker was open. He had locked it, hadn't he? He looked around the change room, but only his friends were there. He grabbed his bag out of the locker and heard something drop to the floor. It was a photograph of Hannah. He flipped the picture over and saw what was written on the back.

I mean it. Stay away from her.

Luke quickly tucked the photo into his bag and got dressed.

"Sorry, guys," he said. "Emergency at the office. Rain check on the beers?"

Whoever wrote this to Luke knew he was still spending time with her, and apparently, this person wasn't going to let up. *Neither am I*, Luke thought.

CHAPTER TWENTY-SEVEN

Luke tried knocking on Hannah's door, but she didn't answer. He decided to check the back since her car was in the driveway. When he unlocked the gate, he saw her sitting on the deck with a book. He walked up to her, and she stood up. He grabbed her by the waist and pulled her in, kissing her intensely. He knew in that moment that he needed her in his life.

"I'm taking you to dinner. You need to eat," he said.

Luke took her to his hockey buddy's restaurant downtown. The owner wasn't there, but Luke knew most of the employees by name. They all treated him very well.

As he and Hannah sat at their table, Luke realized it was his first proper date with her. He felt an urge to impress her, silly as that seemed. When the waiter came, he ordered them a bottle of wine knowing full well that Hannah preferred beer.

But Luke knew his wine, and the gamble paid off. Hannah loved his choice—Luke could see it on her face.

During the meal, it seemed they had both forgotten about their troubles. Luke enjoyed the easy company. If Hannah held on to any of her worry from the night before, she hid it well. She seemed taken by his stories of his childhood.

When the restaurant was almost empty, Luke and Hannah's

plates long since cleared away, Luke went to clear up the bill. He turned to sneak Hannah a smile, but he winced when he noticed the look on her face. Something had shifted in her, and quickly.

She told him she needed to go home. He went over his actions, trying to figure out if he had done something wrong. He tried to grab her hand and she immediately pulled away. He felt like he had lost her. He followed her out to the parking lot and studied her body language. When he noticed her opening the Uber app on her phone, he had to ask. He needed answers.

"Hannah, what's going on? One minute you were fine, and now . . . If something's wrong, let me help you."

She demanded to see his phone. Luke obeyed, unlocking it for her as he passed it over. He needed to gain her trust back. He couldn't handle the feeling of her being upset with him.

As she tapped around, Hannah relaxed. Whatever she was looking for, she didn't find it in his phone.

Hannah didn't explain herself with words. Instead, she pulled out her phone and showed Luke her most recent text message.

Did you enjoy the chocolates? You look beautiful tonight.

Suddenly, Luke felt a rush of anger course through his body. Whoever this person was, they were going to regret messing with Hannah.

"Let's go, Hannah. I'll take you home."

Hannah nodded and followed Luke to his car.

After he had closed the passenger door behind Hannah, Luke went around to his side and got in. Then, he just sat there. The person who had been threatening him and the one who had been harassing Hannah were one and the same—that much he was convinced. How far would this person go? They had already been in Luke's home, had followed him to the hockey arena, and had watched him and Hannah at dinner. Where did it end?

Hannah put her head on Luke's lap and apologized for doubting him. He realized he was clenching his fists and tried to relax.

"Don't be sorry. I'm not upset. Not at you," he said. He hoped she believed him.

Luke asked Hannah to stay with him—he didn't like the idea of her home alone with some maniac stalking about. She declined, and Luke surrendered. Now was not the time to be forceful.

But at least he could see her safely home.

Luke started the car and pulled out of the parking lot, Hannah still lying in his lap. He was going to ask her to put her seatbelt on, but he didn't want to push her away. Not now.

Moments later, he wished he had.

Not a block away from the restaurant, a black coupe sped through the intersection right ahead of Luke's car. He slammed on his brakes, flinging Hannah forward. His car skidded to a stop at the other side of the lights. "Jesus! What the hell—Hannah, are you alright?"

"I think so," she said. "What happened?"

"Some psycho just ran a red in front of us. Black car. Didn't get the . . ." Then, Luke remembered the first time Hannah had accused him. Her brother's stalker had been following him in a black BMW. And whoever texted Hannah only minutes ago would have been at the restaurant. "Wait, do you think—"

"Follow him," Hannah said. She sat up and buckled in.

Luke pulled a quick U-turn and whipped down the road the other car was headed down. Risking a ticket, he ignored the speed limit. If there was a chance to catch this person, Luke didn't want to miss it.

But the roads of downtown Victoria splintered off in more and more possible directions the farther they drove. Eventually they hit a red light. That car could have gone anywhere by then. It was time to give up.

When he stopped in front of Hannah's home, Luke practically begged Hannah to change her mind and stay with him. She declined, and Luke knew there was no arguing with her. Instead, he just kissed her goodnight.

PART THREE

CHAPTER TWENTY-EIGHT

Hannah was exhausted both mentally and physically. She felt like she had just worked a double shift at the hospital. On top of that, she was battered and sore. Luckily, her head wasn't hit very hard. That wouldn't show. But her rib and her knee—she was pretty sure those would bruise.

Hannah decided she needed another day off work. Gauging from her manager's comments when she went home early that Monday, it wouldn't be a hard sell. She called and, sure enough, met with no resistance. Word must have gotten around that she was so out of sorts, and her department took resident burnout pretty seriously.

She decided to have a bath to calm herself down before going to sleep. At the very least, it would ease the inevitable stiffness in her neck the next morning.

Hannah drew herself a bubble bath and soaked in the hot water. She closed her eyes and felt the water move through the spaces between her fingers. It did help a little, but she realized she couldn't soak for long. She was already fighting to keep her eyes open.

Hannah dragged herself out of the bath, drained the water, and dried herself off. She then staggered off to bed, texted Luke goodnight, and put her phone on the charger.

She must have drifted off, because when she saw him standing in the doorway she knew it had to be a dream. Hunter looked at her and smiled. She was so tired. She smiled back at him.

"I miss you, Hannah." His voice sounded so real.

"Why were you on the boat, Hunter?" Hannah asked.

Ignoring her, he spoke once more. "You need to stay away from the man with the green eyes." It was like her last dream of Hunter, but . . . Hannah thought his tone was different this time. It wasn't a warning, was it? It sounded more like a threat.

"What do you mean? Hunter, what's going to happen?" There were so many things she wanted to know; she needed to know.

He walked backwards and closed the bedroom door behind him.

*   *   *

Hannah slept until late morning. As expected, she was sore all over. She sat up and stretched, testing her muscles. When she saw the closed bedroom door, she immediately remembered her dream.

Hannah hadn't slept with the door closed ever since Hunter died. Was her brother alive? Was he in the house?

Hannah knew this was irrational, but she was in no place for logic. The dream she had now seemed more like a memory. His smile, his shape, his voice . . . they had all seemed so real.

Before she could fly out of bed to search for him, her doctor brain started to kick in.

She only saw him because that's what she had wanted to see. He was dead—gone. She convinced herself it was just a dream. But still, the bedroom door sat closed in evidence. If not Hunter, who? The windows were closed, so it wasn't a breeze, and Hannah hadn't been *that* rattled the night before. Not enough to suddenly break a year-old habit without a thought.

Hannah eased herself out of bed and grabbed a robe. It was silly, she reminded herself, to cover up when nobody else could be there. But the thought didn't stop her from doing it.

Finally, Hannah opened the door and crept out into the hallway. A few steps further, and she peeked into Hunter's room.

She made a noise halfway between a scream and a yelp. All of Hunter's things were packed up. The furniture was bare, and stacks of cardboard boxes sat against the wall.

Hannah ran into the kitchen to grab a knife.

Once her breathing had slowed a little, she inched back towards Hunter's room. Her eyes darted around for signs of movement. Carefully, she stepped in. Nobody behind the door or under the bed. She laid her hand on the closet doorknob, twisted, and flung the door open.

Empty.

Hannah searched the rest of the house carefully. When not one hiding spot remained unchecked, she stepped into a pair of sneakers and circled the outside of the house, knife still in hand.

Satisfied at least that she was alone, she returned the knife to the kitchen.

Hannah felt sick to her stomach. Who knew where they had gone, but *someone* had been in her house that night. She texted Luke to tell him she changed her mind—that she wanted to stay with him. He would likely be at work, but Hannah was sure he'd welcome her.

Then, she raced to her bedroom closet and grabbed a suitcase. She gathered enough of her things for a couple of days away and stuffed them inside. At the top of the pile she put her laptop and Hunter's journal.

After she walked out the front door, Hannah locked it and pinched her arm as usual. When she did, she realized how pointless and silly it was. If they wanted in, they were getting in.

Chapter Twenty-Nine

Luke woke up the next morning to the sound of his doorbell. It felt like he had barely slept, so he checked his phone to see what time it was: just after six o'clock. A dull light was just starting to pour in underneath the window shade. Luke pulled on his housecoat and made his way downstairs. When he opened the door, there was no one there.

He looked down and saw a piece of paper tucked under the corner of his welcome mat. When he picked it up, Luke noticed it was the same kind of paper he had found under his wiper blade—lined notebook paper, cut cleanly along the left edge. It had writing on both sides.

Luke looked around, but no one was there. He went back inside and locked the front door behind him. He went to the kitchen and read the words that were written on front of the paper.

August 22, 2017

I had a feeling it was someone I knew. Someone close to me. But I would have never thought it was him. *What does he want from me? And why now?*

I do know one thing: knowing his identity hasn't made it any less unsettling. If anything, it's made everything so much more . . . real. He knows things about me that nobody else does.

This has to stop. I need to talk to him.

Luke turned the paper over to read the other side.

You're next.

Luke could feel the blood rush out of his face. This confirmed it. Everything fit. The shady man he had seen at the beach, the person who had been threatening him and stalking Hannah—they were definitely the same man. But who was it?

The page must have been from Hannah's brother's journal. *From Hunter Melbrook's journal*, Luke thought, remembering the newspaper article about the drowned man. So whoever had been stalking Hunter was someone he knew. Someone who probably knew a lot about Hannah as well. Luke pushed the danger to himself aside. He wouldn't be able to forgive himself if something happened to her.

He paced around the kitchen, and every few minutes he would read the page again. Each time he read it, he grew angrier inside.

On one of his furious rounds, Luke caught sight of the clock on the microwave. Over an hour had passed since he found the message, and his alarm to wake him for work would ring in a few minutes.

In a practical sense, Luke didn't need to be at work for a certain time. He had no meetings scheduled. Still, the quicker he got his job done, the quicker he could visit Hannah. He wanted to be near her more than anything.

Luke folded the paper, went to stuff it in his wallet, then got ready for work.

*   *   *

Hannah couldn't go straight to Luke's house—he wouldn't be home, and she didn't have a key. Instead, she headed to the coffee shop to burn some time.

On the drive over, she kept glancing at her rear-view mirror to make sure she wasn't being followed. She saw her reflection once and noticed her hair was a mess. Of course it was. She had left the house in such a rush, she hadn't bothered to do herself up.

When she parked near the coffee shop, she unzipped her suitcase to grab her laptop and a hairbrush to stuff into her purse. Then, she made a beeline to the bathroom.

At the counter, Hannah was tempted to order a hazelnut latte. Truth be told, it's what she was in the mood for. But she stopped herself. She didn't want to go through the same ordeal as the last time she visited—and the same barista was behind the counter yet again. Instead, she ordered her usual black tea. Balancing her muffin and her drink on her laptop, she found a table as far from the windows as possible and took a seat.

Hannah sat there for hours, keeping her mind distracted with social media feeds and medical journals. She sent the barista away whenever she came to ask if there was anything else Hannah needed. What she needed was to be left alone.

Eventually, Hannah ran out of interesting things to read, and her mind returned to Hunter. Whether what she had seen that night was real or a dream, he was connected to her current situation somehow. That much was clear.

She decided to pick up where she left off three nights before. That Heavy Anchors cruise line had something to do with her brother's death. Even if they no longer existed, they had to have left her something to follow.

Hannah entered *Heavy Anchors Co.* into the search bar of her browser and scanned the results. There was little to be found, but Hannah finally came across an article from a local newspaper's website. The headline read, *Local cruise line issuing refunds.*

Chartered cruise start-up Heavy Anchors Co. must be in it deep because, as of this week, they have cancelled all scheduled bookings and begun issuing refunds to their customers.

The owners couldn't be reached for comment, but one of their clients stated that no reason has been provided for the cancellations.

"They just returned the cheque, and that was the end of it," he

said. "I'm just as baffled as you are."

The rest of the article was no more helpful. Still, an event like that would be big news in the boating industry. Surely Hannah's father knew something about it. Why wouldn't he admit it?

Unfortunately, that article was all Hannah could find. When her laptop battery gave out, so did she. She still had her phone, but what was the point? This angle obviously wasn't getting her anywhere.

She needed to look elsewhere. Lacking any clear direction, she decided to go to the place where it all began—where everything was lost. She drove towards the water.

Chapter Thirty

For the second time that week, Luke finished his work early. It turned out the office was a better distraction than he'd thought. By early afternoon, he had not only finished his website updates but also the articles he'd given up on during the weekend. It helped to know he'd see Hannah that night, and he knew they would both be safer in each other's company.

With nothing more to do, Luke told James he was taking off early. "Must be nice," James said. "Well, go on. But next time, you're telling me about your lady before you get to leave."

"My 'lady'?"

"C'mon, buddy. It's my leg that's busted up, not my brain. I can tell you've been different ever since that night at the bar. You found her, didn't you?"

Luke answered with a smirk and left the office. If only James knew how complicated it really was.

On the way home, Luke stopped at the grocery store. He wanted to make Hannah a nice dinner to make her feel at home. As he loaded his shopping cart, he kept thinking to himself how much he wanted and needed to get to know her better. There were so many things about her he didn't know.

Luke pulled into the driveway and unlocked his trunk to unload the groceries. On his way to the back of the car, he noticed another black BMW parked down the street. He took off towards the vehicle in an instant. He didn't know what he'd do when he got there, only that he wasn't wasting this chance. He hadn't realized how deep his anger went until that moment.

As he approached the car, it began to drive away. Luke tried to keep up with it, but it sped off too quickly. He stood in the middle of the street and his brain finally caught up with his body. Sure, that car looked like the one he had almost hit the night before, but what if it wasn't? What if he just scared the daylights out of some poor bystander who just happened to have the misfortune of driving the wrong car? What if he had actually *caught* this person?

Luke was scared of the answer. He was done being reckless. Before he acted, he needed to know who he was dealing with—with absolute certainty.

* * *

Hannah grabbed a blanket out of her trunk and walked towards the beach. The tide was coming in, so she picked a spot near the treeline and sat, looking out at the water. The place where Hunter's body had been found was now well underwater.

Hannah gazed outwards and tried to put the facts together. Her thoughts ran in circles as she watched the waves roll in and out. Every once in a while, the water would just touch her feet before making its way back to its home in the vast openness of the ocean.

After a while, Hannah had a strange feeling. She pulled her legs in, wrapping her arms around them, and looked around the beach. Then, she saw—she was being watched.

He was quite far away, but she could have sworn it was him. Hunter. Hannah remembered her dream again. There was no way he was real. Her mind was playing tricks on her. She was tired. Hungry. Stressed out. There was no way.

Carefully, Hannah stood and folded her blanket, keeping an

eye on the figure. She backed away. After a few steps, her ankle hit something solid—a piece of driftwood—and she almost tripped. As soon as she recovered her balance, she turned and bolted to her car.

When she was safe inside and her doors were locked, she played with the ring hanging from her necklace as she tried to comprehend what she had seen. She knew this wasn't possible. She knew her brother was gone. They had a funeral and said goodbye to him. They buried him in the ground. His death was in the papers. Hannah was frightened that she really had lost it for good.

When something wet hit her hand, Hannah noticed she was crying. She sat for a while and let the tears come, not bothering to wipe them away.

CHAPTER THIRTY-ONE

The moment Hannah saw Luke, it felt like everything was going to be alright. Part of her resisted that feeling of safety—she didn't know if she could trust her own feelings anymore. The dominant part of her, though, let herself just enjoy the comfort of his company. It was exactly what she needed, and she didn't want to spoil it.

Luke had dinner ready for Hannah's arrival. She could smell it the second Luke opened the door. *He's so sweet*, she thought.

Luke went in for an embrace and Hannah jumped up, wrapping her legs around his waist. He held her up as they kissed. She never wanted to stop. His face was getting stubbly again, but Hannah ignored the scratchiness. It looked sexy on him—almost as sexy as the thought of him working away in the kitchen.

Luke lowered Hannah to the floor, but she couldn't take her eyes off him. Hannah was consumed by this man. Through everything that was happening to her, he was the only thing that felt right. Not only right. Luke felt perfect.

Hannah finally turned her eyes away. She wondered what their story would have been like if they had met under normal circumstances. She wondered why he would want to be with someone with so much baggage.

Luke kissed her nose gently, seemingly sensing her mood.

"Let's go eat. Dinner is out on the deck." He gently guided Hannah through the kitchen and out the door.

Hannah was impressed by Luke's attention to detail. The table was covered with a spotless tablecloth, and the plates were covered with lids to keep the food warm. The cutlery was neatly arranged. He had put a couple of beer bottles in a small ice bucket.

She turned to him, her hand raised to her mouth. Luke beamed and led her to her seat.

The food tasted even better than it smelled.

"This is incredible," Hannah said.

Luke smiled and uncapped a bottle of beer for her.

They ate in comfortable silence under the warm sun, trading affectionate glances and occasionally touching hands. *This is what love is like*, Hannah thought. *I had nearly forgotten.*

* * *

When their meal was finished, Luke stood and started clearing away the dishes. Hannah started to get up to help, but Luke put a hand out. "I'll take care of it," he said. "Just relax." Hannah got settled again and sipped on the remainder of her beer.

Luke loaded the dishes into the dishwasher then headed upstairs. In the master bathroom, he lit some candles and drew a bubble bath. If Hannah's day had been anything like his, she could use one. And not only that—he could take some time to do a little research.

When the bath was filled, Luke returned to Hannah. She was finished her beer and leaning against the railing, staring into the sky as the sun set. *I wonder what she's thinking*, he thought. He didn't ask.

"Come with me," Luke said. He put his hand under Hannah's arm then led her inside and up the stairs. He could see Hannah blush as he took her into his room. Then, he noticed a slight change in her bearing when he opened the bathroom door and showed her to the bath. Was it relief? Gratitude? Or maybe disappointment?

"I left work early today," he said, "so I have a bit of catching up to do. I'll be just downstairs. Let me know if you need anything."

Hannah nodded. "Thanks, Luke."

"Anything," he repeated. He kissed her on the cheek then left her alone, closing the door behind him.

With Hannah in the bath, Luke went down to the living room couch and opened his laptop. First, there was something he needed to know for sure. He typed *Hannah* in the Facebook search bar and then—remembering the drowned man's name—added *Melbrook*.

That was her alright.

Luke poked around Hannah's page for a few minutes. Before long, he found a photo of her with her brother. They were geared up with hiking boots and backpacks, all smiles and arms around shoulders. Hannah's friend Adam was tagged in the photo too, but he wasn't shown. *Must have been holding the camera*, Luke decided.

Luke remembered back to his childhood. He and his father used to go on hikes when Luke was little—long before his father died. Though Luke never took the time to explore the wilderness as an adult, he had a fondness for the memories. His father would always try to turn their hikes into lessons. Luke could still remember some of them.

Look! See that, Luke? his father had said, pointing to a salmon jumping out of the river.

Oh! What's it doing? Luke asked.

It's swimming upstream. There's another one!

The young Luke watched for more, but no more salmon shot out of the water like the other two had. Soon, he lost interest and started walking again.

Luke's father put his hand on Luke's shoulder, holding him back. *Why do you think they do that?* he said.

I dunno, Luke replied.

Always ask questions, Luke. Think about the big picture. The more you find out about the world, the more things will start to make sense.

Luke had thought about this for a moment, then nodded obediently.

Remember, Luke. Always think about the why. Now, tell me. What do you think they swim upstream for?

The answer itself wasn't important. Luke had gotten it wrong, but his father was still proud of him for thinking logically. Luke needed to think that way now. He needed to think about the why. Why did that man kill Hunter? Why did he want Luke to stay away from Hannah? Was there something Luke didn't know about Hannah and her family? What was he missing? He continued to ask himself question after question.

Luke closed his laptop and got up from the couch. He needed to see the big picture. He needed to go back to the place where it happened.

If I'm lucky, Luke thought, *I might even be followed.*

CHAPTER THIRTY-TWO

The temperature was just right. The bubbles were thick, just the way she liked it. She grabbed her phone off the ledge and checked her text messages, careful not to drop the phone into the water.

Tawn had sent her a couple of messages since morning. *Get well soon!* the first said. Then, the second, *If you're feeling better, we're going out tonight. You should come!*

The latest message was three hours old. Hannah spent a minute deciding whether she even needed to reply. Guilt eventually persuaded her.

Hannah: Sorry, been in bed most of the day. I'll see you tomorrow. Have fun!

Tawn replied with two messages in practically no time at all.

Tawn: That's okay. Next time!

Tawn: *Adam has been asking about you. Think he's jealous? ;)*

This took Hannah by surprise. Adam had barely spoken a word to her for over a year and a half. Why was he interested again all of a sudden?

Hannah couldn't think of anything to say to this, so she backed out of the conversation. Below Tawn's name was the message from the night before. Hannah stared at it for a few moments.

An idea sprang to her mind. She had his number—why couldn't

she just call? Whoever sent that message owed her some answers.

Hannah hit dial and held the phone up to her ear, her heart racing. Part of her hoped to hear her brother's voice on the other end. Another part of her feared it.

After one ring, the call went straight to voice mail. Hannah hung up before the robotic voice could finish. She was equal parts disappointed and relieved. What would she have said if he answered?

Hannah got out of the tub and got dressed. Luke had left his closet open, and Hannah took this as an invitation to borrow a bathrobe, which she put on overtop of her pajamas before heading downstairs. She called for Luke. When he didn't answer, she searched each room for him. Finally, she noticed a note on the kitchen counter.

Had to run out to get more printer ink. Be back soon.

Hannah took a deep breath. *Even in his own home I can't get him to stay put.* At least, she decided, she was safer in his house. Still, she felt lonely.

She made herself some tea and grabbed Hunter's journal out of her suitcase while the tea steeped. With journal and tea in hand, she sank into Luke's puffy grey couch. She started reading again.

Hannah avoided the pages where Hunter had written about his stalker. She avoided the entries about Hunter's stressful time at the hospital. She wanted to read about his happy memories.

Most of the happy memories were about Nicole.

Who was this woman? Hannah thought. She noticed her imagination had created a substitute for Nicole: the woman from her dream. The woman in the white gown. The one who stood on the boat and held a glass of champagne, laughing. *No, that won't do.*

Hannah pulled out her phone to look Nicole up on Facebook. It was only fair to imagine her as she really was.

Hunter's page was, of course, still active. Hannah didn't know if she could ever bring herself to have it deleted. She had barely even looked at it since he died. She just hadn't been ready.

His wall was full of tributes and memories from his friends, family, and acquaintances. After scrolling through for a few moments, Hannah went to his friends list. There, she found only one Nicole who lived in Victoria. She tapped on the name—and was shocked when Nicole's picture loaded onto her screen.

Her imagination had been right. She looked *exactly* like the woman from her dream. But how could that be possible? How could she have dreamt of Nicole when they hadn't ever met? Hannah tried to think of where else she might have seen this woman. Hunter hadn't introduced them—he said so himself in his journal. She tried to think if she had seen her at the hospital or at the coffee shop. No matter how hard she tried, she could not remember seeing this woman outside of her dreams.

It had been over an hour and Luke still wasn't home, but Hannah was getting tired. She headed upstairs and grabbed her suitcase from the guestroom, bringing it to Luke's bedroom. When he got home, she wanted to know. When he fell asleep, she wanted to be next to him.

She snuggled into Luke's king-sized bed and tucked herself under the goose-down feather duvet. It was the most comfortable bed she had ever been in, but it was still missing something. She hoped that something wouldn't be missing for long.

*   *   *

Luke sat by the water for a long time, running through his memory over and over again. The drowned man—Hunter—had been wearing a life jacket, but it hadn't saved him. Did the second man know Hunter was already dead? Or had he gone there to finish him off? And when he found Luke there, what was going through his mind?

Luke wondered why that man hadn't pursued him. He wouldn't want any witnesses, would he? But he stayed at the edge of the trees as if he was afraid to touch the sand.

That was it, Luke decided. The man didn't want to leave foot-prints. Without a witness, he could have disposed of the body and nobody would ever know what became of Hunter. Luke compli-cated things. That's why the man had looked so furious at Luke. That's why he didn't follow.

But still, why had he wanted Hunter dead in the first place? Who was he, and what did he have to gain? Luke recounted the facts. This man was someone Hunter knew—someone he knew well. This man had left Luke alone until after he started spending time with Hannah.

The memory hit Luke like a sack of bricks.

I know you're here to see Hannah. That's cool. But there's something I should tell you.

He knew Hunter well. *He* barely let Hannah out of his sight when they went to the club together. Luke wanted to slap himself for not suspecting *him* sooner.

Luke decided he'd had enough of the beach. Besides, his excuse of leaving to get printer ink would be wearing thin. He walked back to his car and wondered what to do about the new lead.

When Luke pulled up to his house, he noticed that most of the lights were still off downstairs. Careful not to make too much noise, he settled onto the couch with his laptop. Then, he turned on the television and started looking through Hunter's Facebook page again.

Luke had found Adam's page and just started looking around when he saw her figure come around the corner. Quickly exiting the browser, he turned to Hannah. She looked worried.

"What's the matter, Hannah?" Luke said.

"I had another nightmare."

Luke gave Hannah a sympathetic look and signalled for her to sit on the couch with him. She went over and put her head on his lap.

"Why are you still up?" she asked.

"I'm just catching up on work. I didn't want to wake you up." Luke gently stroked her hair as he stared at the desktop image on his computer. Soon, she was fast asleep.

CHAPTER THIRTY-THREE

Luke must have carried Hannah up to bed because she woke up next to him. She kissed him on the shoulder, but he didn't wake. He had probably stayed up late. Leaving work early to have dinner ready must have set him back a fair bit.

Hannah wasn't much of a cook, but she wanted to return the favour. She decided to go to the café to get them some coffee and breakfast. It was something at least.

She got ready and grabbed her car keys. As she moved Hunter's journal into her purse, her phone went off. *Just my alarm,* she thought. She clicked the button on the side of her phone to silence it. She still had plenty of time to get to the café and back.

But when she reached her car, she noticed something tucked under her windshield wiper. It was another note—like the one she had found in her locker. She swallowed hard as she read the words.

Why won't you listen to me, Hannah?

Hannah stuffed the note into her purse and got into her car. She locked the doors and looked around. There was no one to be seen. She took off to the café as quickly as she could. She wanted to get back to Luke. She knew that she could trust Luke. She knew she was safe with Luke.

Or was she? Hannah had assumed the man who was following

her wouldn't find her at Luke's, but he had. Was there anywhere she would be safe?

After Hannah got the coffee and bagels, she sat in the parking lot with her windows rolled down. She pulled the note out from her purse, moving her phone aside. It was then that she noticed: she had a missed call. The ringing hadn't been her alarm after all—she had forgotten to set it. All her call history said was *No Caller ID*.

He hadn't only been at Luke's house—he knew when Hannah was leaving. Maybe he was still there waiting for her. Hannah wasn't about to find out. She drove straight to the hospital without a second thought.

Chapter Thirty-Four

When Hannah opened her locker to grab her spare scrubs, she ignored the note and the copy of her ring. She just wanted to pretend it was a normal day. The hospital would be too busy for anything to bother her.

At least, that's how it should have been. First thing that morning, Hannah had been scheduled to handle a minor surgery under her attending's supervision, but he sent her away. "Just take it easy today," he said. "You still don't look well."

Hannah protested, but he wouldn't hear any of it. Instead, he gave her a list of patients to gather old medical records for. When she finished that, he had another resident send her on odd jobs. The attending hadn't treated her that way since her intern year. Now Hannah knew how Hunter must have felt.

Just before Hannah's lunch break, the attending sent her to check on Chris Walsh—the patient she was supposed to operate on that morning. The assignment bothered her more than she knew it should have. But how was she supposed to feel? The attending hadn't even let her watch the procedure.

She walked into Chris's room to find him sound asleep. The work was exceptionally done, of course. She checked the patient's vitals on the monitor at the edge of the bed and put a handout on the tray table, which contained education on dressing changes and scar management. The nurses would review this with the patient once the doctor cleared him for discharge.

With that finished, Hannah was ready to take her break. But before she left the room, the patient stirred. Hannah paused and heard him mumbling something.

"Sorry, what did you say?" she asked.

"Saw your brother this morning," Chris said.

Hannah froze and stared at him.

"Or your cousin, maybe. Looked an awful lot like you."

"What do you mean he looked like me?" Hannah asked.

"Shorter hair, stronger face, but could have been your twin." He was wide awake now and not the least bit delirious.

"Uh, thank you for . . ." Hannah searched for the words, but that was all she could say before her legs carried her out the room.

Hannah tried to calm herself down as she took her lunch. She took small bites of her cafeteria sandwich, thumbing the pages of Hunter's journal. There wasn't much more for her to find in it, but it had become a sort of security blanket. There was more of Hunter in those pages then there had ever been in the ring hanging from her necklace.

After twenty minutes, she put the half-eaten sandwich down. Had Hunter really been at the hospital, or had she imagined the whole exchange with Chris? Her brother couldn't have been there, could he? Even if he were alive, someone would have recognized him.

No, Hannah decided. *I'm just losing my mind after all.* She sighed and put the journal back in her purse then dumped the remainder of the sandwich in the garbage.

As soon as Hannah made it back to her department, she heard her name on the intercom. She was wanted at reception. *Who could that be?* she wondered. *Maybe Luke came to visit me.*

Or maybe it's Hunter again.

It was neither. Waiting by reception was the woman from

Hannah's dreams. She had seen her again that night. It was Nicole.

In her dream, Nicole was drowning. Hannah dove in to save her, but when she reached the spot where Nicole had been, she was nowhere to be found. Hannah instead found herself in Nicole's white gown. The black water weighed on the fabric and pulled Hannah into its depths.

"You're her, aren't you? You're Hannah." Nicole's voice brought Hannah back to the present.

"Yeah, that's . . . Could you hold on a second?" Hannah left Nicole where she was standing and went over to the receptionist.

Hannah leaned in and whispered, "You can *see* her, right?" She pointed her eyes meaningfully towards Nicole.

The receptionist recoiled a little and scrunched her eyebrows. She nodded slightly. "Is everything okay?"

"Yeah. It's fine." Hannah headed back over to Nicole. "Hi. Sorry about that. Should we go somewhere to talk?"

"I don't have much time," Nicole said, "but I wanted to bring you this." She pulled a small plastic bag out of her purse and gave it to Hannah.

Inside was Hannah's grandfather's pocket watch. She recognized it instantly. Hunter had taken really good care of it.

"Where did you get this?" Hannah asked.

"I'm sorry. Hunter left it at my place, and I didn't want to . . . I mean, it's been almost a year, and I'm sure your family . . . I'm really sorry. I should have given it back a long time ago." Nicole wiped the corners of her eyes with her finger.

"It's alright," Hannah said. "I mean, thank you."

"You look so much like him," Nicole said, finally digging a tissue from her purse.

Hannah didn't know what to say next. They both stood in silence for what felt like an eternity.

"I need to get to an appointment, but do you think we could meet for coffee sometime?" Nicole asked.

Hannah could see how charming she was. She understood why her brother loved this woman. She was kind-hearted and understanding. Hannah could tell all of this in a matter of moments.

"Of course," Hannah said. "I'd really like that."

They exchanged numbers and went their separate ways.

Chapter Thirty-Five

Before the end of her shift, Hannah ran into Tawn.

"There you are!" Tawn said. "I've been keeping an eye out for you all day!"

Hannah sighed. "It's been quite a day."

"No kidding. You look pretty tired. You missed another great night, but I'm glad you're feeling a little better." Tawn went in for a hug. "Hey, you know what we should do? We should go get some ice cream! It's been forever."

Tawn was right. She, Hannah, and Hunter used to go for ice cream after work together at least once a week. It had been months since Tawn had even bothered to ask. Hannah must have really looked like she could use it.

That was half of the truth. The other half was that Hannah just didn't have the energy to come up with an excuse.

"Alright," said Hannah. "I'll meet you there."

When Hannah arrived at the old ice cream shop they used to visit, Tawn was already sitting on top of a picnic table eating a black cherry ice cream in a waffle cone. Tawn always had something different. If they came out with a new flavour every week, she would still try every last one.

Hannah walked up to Tawn and gave her a loose hug, avoiding

the hand holding the ice cream. She ordered herself a coffee-flavoured one as usual then joined Tawn on the table.

They didn't say much until their cones were finished. Something was missing, and Hannah could tell they both knew it.

Tawn told Hannah about a date she went on with the German man. His name was Kurt. She was still seeing him, which surprised Hannah a little. Usually Tawn would have moved on to someone else by now with her dating track record. Maybe there was more to this relationship than Hannah initially thought. Hannah felt a bit guilty for being so quick to judge.

With her own story out of the way, Tawn looked Hannah in the eyes.

"Are you doing okay?" Tawn said.

Hannah took a moment, then she just nodded.

"A year this weekend, isn't it? I know I wouldn't be handling it very well. This week must have been hard." When Hannah didn't reply, Tawn continued. "But I'm proud of you for coming out with us on your birthday weekend. It's nice to sort of have you back. I missed you."

Hannah wasn't used to this sort of attention from Tawn. She knew Tawn cared about her, but she hadn't really shown it like this. Even when Hunter died, she just avoided the topic altogether like she wanted to help Hannah forget.

Hannah was tired of crying, but she couldn't help herself.

Tawn put her arm over Hannah's shoulder.

"You know, you should take a vacation. Maybe visit your parents. I think they'd be happy to see you right about now."

Hannah nodded again. Even though Tawn didn't know the half of it, she was right.

When they said their goodbyes and went back to their cars, Hannah called the hospital. She was prepared for a negotiation, but they surprised her by giving her a week off—effective immediately. The evening manager seemed relieved Hannah was actually using some of her vacation time.

After that, Hannah booked a flight to Vancouver for Saturday morning. Friday was available as well, but she wanted a chance to meet with Nicole before leaving. Nicole seemed glad to hear from her so soon and agreed to see her for coffee the following afternoon.

She had just started her car when she realized she had almost forgotten to tell her parents she was coming. Hannah shut the engine off and called them. She didn't get to speak with her father, but her mother sounded thrilled.

Work: check. Flight: check. Parents: check.

All that remained was for Hannah to return home to pack.

But she wasn't about to go alone.

CHAPTER THIRTY-SIX

Hannah had told Luke she was going to be a little late getting back after work, so he waited for her on the front porch and enjoyed a cold beer in the sun. He had a lot on his mind, but seeing Hannah again was quickly becoming the highlight of his day. He wanted to see her the moment she arrived.

Still, Hannah took longer than he expected. After waiting for almost an hour, he started to get worried. A dangerous man was keeping an eye on her. Could something have happened?

To his relief, she finally pulled into his driveway just as he was about to call her. He stood and greeted her with a kiss.

"I'm taking some time off work," she said.

"That's great! We could—"

"And I'm going to visit my parents."

"Oh," Luke said. He looked down at her feet. "So, when are you leaving?"

"Saturday. You can come with me! I'm sure they wouldn't mind, and there were still seats left when I booked my flight."

Luke considered this for a moment. The idea of a weekend away with Hannah was tempting, but he had business with a certain someone. He couldn't waste the chance to settle things with Hannah out of harm's way.

Hannah seemed to sense his hesitation. "If you think it's still too soon to meet my parents, that's okay. I guess it's a little much after only a week."

The thought of meeting Hannah's parents didn't bother Luke at all. Still, it was the most convenient excuse. "Yeah. Maybe next time."

"But . . ." Hannah bit her lip. "Could you come with me to my place? While I pack, I mean. I don't have everything I need."

"Of course! No problem. We can grab dinner on the way back."

Luke started his car while Hannah ran up to grab her suitcase. Then, they were off to Hannah's place.

When they got there, Luke settled onto Hannah's couch. But before he even had time to pull his phone out, a scream came from the hallway. Luke shot up and ran over to Hannah. She was pale and had her hands over her mouth. He glanced around, but nothing unusual caught his eye. Hannah stared into the empty guestroom like she had seen a ghost.

"What's the matter? Did you see something?"

"Gone," was all she said.

"Gone? What's gone?"

"Everything. His things—they were here."

"What do you mean? Your brother's?"

"I never packed his things away—then yesterday it was all boxed up, and now . . ."

So *that's* why she had changed her mind about staying with him. Her home wasn't safe. *He* had been there.

Luke cradled Hannah in his arms and stroked her hair. "It's okay. Let's just get you packed and get out of here."

I have to make all of this stop, Luke thought. *I need to get to the bottom of this.*

By the time Hannah returns from visiting her parents, I'll have done just that.

CHAPTER THIRTY-SEVEN

Hannah spent the following morning pacing around while Luke worked nearby on his laptop. It helped her peace of mind that he had the freedom to work from home, but it wasn't quite enough. She still expected him to take off at any moment. Maybe he would need to grab something from the office. Maybe he had forgotten about an appointment and would need to suddenly run out to make it in time. Maybe something was missing from the recipe he had planned to use for dinner.

Thankfully, Luke stayed put—and when the afternoon came, it was Hannah who had to leave him alone.

Hannah had agreed to meet Nicole at a coffee shop she had never been to. When she got into her car, she mapped the trip on her phone and discovered she hadn't left enough time for the drive.

She drove ten over the speed limit so she wouldn't be late.

Hannah had a knot in her stomach. She was nervous for so many reasons. She was nervous about sitting down and talking to a woman that her brother loved. She was nervous about learning more about her brother and was scared of what she might find out. She was nervous that Nicole might suspect Hannah was losing her mind.

Hannah tried to turn off her thoughts as she walked through the door.

She saw Nicole immediately. She was sitting at table in the corner near the back. She was stunning, and Hannah added inadequacy to her list of reasons to be nervous.

Then, Hannah noticed that Nicole hadn't ordered anything yet. She knew that Nicole had waited for her. It was a small gesture—almost nothing—but it reminded Hannah of what she had decided about Nicole when they met the day before: she was a sincere and thoughtful person. Hannah knew that her brother must have loved her because of the little things she thought of. Things that most people didn't. She couldn't help but wonder if her brother would have married this woman.

Nicole waved at Hannah from across the room. Hannah walked towards her and tried to smile.

"Thank you for meeting me," Hannah said.

Hannah could tell Nicole was holding back feelings of her own. She hadn't ever considered how much other people had been affected by Hunter's death. All this time she felt so alone when there were others who were going through it with her.

"I'm really glad to see you. He told me so much." Nicole's words were calming and genuine. Her eyes smiled as she spoke. She was charming.

Hannah wished she could say she had heard so much about Nicole too. She wished Hunter would have shared that part of his life with her. She hated that everything she knew about Nicole was from a journal written by her dead brother.

They went to the counter together to order their drinks. Hannah was surprised when Nicole asked for a hazelnut latte. Her tribute to Hunter gave Hannah a little courage, and she ordered the same. They smiled at each other when the barista handed them their orders.

Hannah had so many questions; she didn't know where to begin. Nicole sat patiently. She was comfortable with the silence, which was refreshing for Hannah. Since he died, Hannah noticed that people always want to say something to try to make it all better. It was as if they thought she would break like fragile glass in the windows of silence.

Unlike all the awkward silences that came after her companions had run out of things to say, this silence felt peaceful. The only other people Hannah had ever felt this way with were Hunter and Luke.

But it couldn't last forever. They had met to talk.

"I really loved your brother. He meant everything to me. I know we didn't know each other long, but I felt like I had known him my whole life." Nicole wiped a tear from her eye before it could fall down her cheek.

Hannah was taken off guard by what she said. She wasn't sure how to respond. It surprised her how open Nicole was. She was glad that Hunter got the chance to love someone so pure. It was then that Hannah realized why Nicole looked so familiar. She had seen her before—and not just in her dreams.

"You were at the funeral," Hannah said.

Nicole nodded, her lips pressed in a tight line. "I brought the watch with me, but it just never seemed like the right time."

"Who was he meeting on the boat, Nicole?" The question came out before Hannah could think twice.

"What boat?"

"The night he died. He went on a cruise ship to meet someone." Hannah looked her in the eyes to see how Nicole reacted to her words.

Nicole looked utterly confused. She withdrew from the table a little.

"I don't know what you're talking about. I'm sorry, Hannah," Nicole said.

"It was in his journal. The night before he died, he said he was going out to . . ." Hannah stopped herself before she said too much.

"He never told me . . . We were at the Mexican restaurant by the pier having dinner. He was going to take me to the gala and introduce us, but he changed his mind last minute."

Hannah could see that Nicole was trying to hold back tears.

"He just said he didn't want to go anymore. He was acting a little strange, but he did that from time to time, so I never thought to press him about it. He told me that he was going to just head home and that he wanted to walk." A tear streamed down her cheek, followed by another. She quickly wiped them away from her face with her finger.

"So you last saw him at the restaurant? Did you talk to him after that, or was that the last time you spoke to him?" Hannah could tell she was making Nicole uncomfortable, but she needed to understand.

"I left the restaurant and texted him when I got home to see if he got back to his place." She paused for a moment and tried to compose herself. "He never texted me back."

Hannah could tell that Nicole blamed herself. In that, she was in good company.

Nicole reached across the table and grabbed Hannah's hand. She caught Hannah with an intense gaze. She leaned in towards Hannah and whispered something that made the hairs on Hannah's arms stand up.

"Sometimes I still see him."

Hannah pulled away and sat in silence, staring at the girl across from her.

"I'm sorry, I know that sounds crazy." Nicole stood and handed Hannah a business card from her purse. "Stay in touch, okay?" She gave Hannah a hug.

Hannah wanted to ask her what she had meant by that. Instead, she just watched Nicole walk away.

CHAPTER THIRTY-EIGHT

On Saturday morning, Luke woke up early to make Hannah a big breakfast. When they finished, he loaded her suitcase into the trunk of his BMW and drove her to the airport.

"When do you get back?" he asked as they pulled up to the drop-off area.

"Tuesday," said Hannah. "But I can change my flight if I miss you too much."

Luke smiled and leaned over for a kiss. *That should be enough time to sort this out*, he thought.

Hannah hugged him and kissed him slowly. When she lingered near his lips, all he could think about was how much he loved that woman. He almost changed his mind and booked a flight right then and there.

But soon, Hannah was inside the terminal and Luke was parked nearby. He grabbed his phone and navigated to Adam's Facebook page. By now it was familiar.

Luke sent Adam a message with nothing but his number and the words *call me*. If that strategy didn't work, he could always get Adam's number from Tawn, but he preferred to leave everyone else out of this.

The call came soon after Luke had returned home.

"Hi, Luke. How's it going?"

"We need to talk."

"Oh. Uh, yeah. I think I know what this is about. I'm just on a break right now, but I can stop by in the evening. How's that sound?"

Not even playing dumb about it, Luke thought. *This guy has some nerve.*

"I'll be home," Luke said.

"Alright. Cool. See you then, man."

Not a minute later, Luke's phone buzzed again. Adam had sent him a text message.

Sorry, I forgot to ask for your address.

Like he didn't already know.

CHAPTER THIRTY-NINE

Hannah lined up at the bag check an hour and a half before her flight. She had never liked airports, but this time felt different. Less like a prison intake process. More like an evacuation.

She made it through security quite quickly. Once she had her purse, phone, and headphones back, she found a coffee shop where she could read while she waited to board.

Hannah ordered a black tea and sat at a table overlooking the airplanes getting ready to depart. She opened up the journal and found a page she hadn't yet read.

July 5, 2017

I went to the gym today, and when I got back to my car there was something strange on my windshield. It was a business card with nothing but a phone number and four digits below it. I flipped it over and it had 26.08.17 written in small letters.

I called the number from the parking lot. It was an answering service, and it needed a password. The four digits worked. "You have one new message," it said.

I listened to it: a confirmation for a booking I had never made. But they had my name.

It had to be him.

Hannah read this passage twice. The words felt heavy. She

didn't know for sure if that man had killed her brother, but it was his fault Hunter died. It was his fault she hadn't met Nicole as Hunter's future fiancée but as his grieving girlfriend. His fault Hannah's life was such a mess. A shiver went down her spine and she felt anger build up inside of her.

And now, she was running. But what else could she do? She still didn't know who he was.

Hannah finished her tea and texted Luke to tell him she was about to board the plane and she would miss him.

She found her seat near the back of the plane. She always sat near a window. She liked to watch the sky and the earth below her. She found it peaceful, and she needed that peace more than ever. She put her headphones in, closed her eyes, and rested her head against the window.

Soon, Hannah gathered her things and walked off the plane. She picked up her baggage, thankful that her bag was one of the first to come out. Everyone around her seemed to be moving so fast. Even in the middle of the day, the airport lighting looked cold and artificial.

She left the airport and got into a cab, which took her through a small town. The driver went up a narrow, winding road surrounded by mountains. Her ears popped as the elevation increased. Hannah swallowed hard every few minutes.

When she got to the top of the mountain, she saw a large wooden building surrounded by flowers and trees. She moved like her body knew where to go, pushing through the double oak doors and down a long hallway. There was a lounge to her right. She saw three men having beers in their golf clothes, laughing and smiling. She could have sworn one of the men winked at her.

She walked past the lounge and out to a deserted patio filled with large round tables. The patio overlooked a cliff and a beautiful golf course. Hannah scanned her surroundings. The landscape was dotted with evergreen trees. She could hear the sounds of nature.

Hannah noticed how darkness was starting to take over the day. She sat at one of the tables, then she started to hear voices and laughter, which became louder and louder by the second. Hannah turned around and saw that the remaining tables were now full of people dressed in formal attire. She turned back to face her own table and jumped when she saw all the people sitting with her. They hadn't been there a second ago.

She heard cheering from inside the building. Through a part in the crowd, she watched as a woman walked down the stairs towards the tables. The woman was wearing a beautiful white dress with a large tulle bottom. She was breathtaking.

Shortly after, a man followed. He wore a black suit with a white dress shirt underneath. He kissed the woman's hand and then looked at Hannah, his face emotionless. He stared at her and pointed up at something in the distance behind her.

Hannah turned. She looked up into the night and her mouth dropped open as she read the writing in the sky.

Stay away from the man with the green eyes.

A hand grabbed Hannah's shoulder tightly. She followed the hand with her eyes and looked to see who it belonged to. It was Luke standing over her. His grip tightened on her shoulder. He was hurting her. She tried to shout, but nothing came out.

Hannah woke up to the flight attendant announcing that it was time to prepare for landing. *It wasn't real,* she reminded herself. *You're safe now.*

She got off the plane and headed to claim her baggage, texting her mother while she waited. With her suitcase in hand, she headed towards the taxi loop.

Halfway there, Hannah remembered her dream and changed her mind. She wasn't about to let someone else drive. If she was going somewhere, she would be in control.

Instead, Hannah found the rental car desk.

CHAPTER FORTY

Hannah drove north through the city then turned down the highway. There were thick trees surrounding the road. She rolled the window down and enjoyed the fresh air.

Finally, she saw the sign for the turnoff. Hannah had only visited her parents' new house twice, but she still remembered to turn after the white picket fence. She saw the fence approaching ahead and turned right. The house was only a little way in from there.

They lived in a bungalow on a half-acre lot. It had been a new build—not large, but beautiful. Hannah always wondered if they chose to build a house to distract themselves. They lived in a small rental home near the edge of the city until their place was ready for them to move into.

As Hannah pulled up the driveway, she immediately noticed that there were no flowers planted in the pots. Her mother used to always buy a ton of flowers as soon as spring hit and would spend days planting them. Maybe she didn't have the time anymore now that she rarely spent any time at home.

Hannah left her suitcase in the car and walked up to the front door, knocking gently. Her mother opened the door while she was still knocking.

"Hi, Hannah bear!" her mother said as she gave Hannah a big hug.

"Hi, mom," Hannah replied with a smile.

Hannah scanned the house as her mother ushered her in. She remembered why she never felt comfortable there. The house itself was beautiful, but it was so bare. She thought back to their house growing up and how there would be pictures and stuffed animals in every room. It was a warm and welcoming place, and she missed it deeply. It held so many memories of their lives together—back when their family was perfect and unbroken.

"Where's Dad?" Hannah asked.

"Oh, he's in the basement. Glued to some war documentary as usual," her mother answered.

It hurt a little that her father hadn't come to the door to greet her. She wondered if he was avoiding her. *Well, he'll come up when he's ready.*

Her mother led her into the kitchen and started making some tea. She put two cups on the table with cream and sugar in them. Hannah used to always have tea with her mother on her days off. They would catch up on Hannah's life and laugh about things that Hannah and Hunter would do as children. Her mother would always say how much of a handful it was having twins.

Hannah's mother poured the tea into their cups and sat down. Hannah hadn't noticed it at first, but she saw something in her mother's movements and her expression. She looked drained. It seemed like she was fighting to keep moving as her body screamed for her to stop. Dark circles lined her lower eyelids—the same circles Hannah had seen in her own reflection.

Her mother gave her updates about her family. She told Hannah about how her cousin Alexis had gotten engaged and how her aunt had taken control of planning the entire wedding. Hannah noticed that her mother wouldn't allow even seconds of dead air to take over. She just kept talking and talking.

Hannah's mother walked up to the fridge and returned with a card that had been pinned there with a magnet—an invitation of some sort. At first Hannah thought it was the invite to her cousin's wedding. Her mother slid it across the table. "Take a look at this," she said.

Hannah brought it closer to her face. It was a black invitation with gold foil writing across the top. It said *Masquerade Party* on the front above a picture of an intricate mask. Hannah turned it over and saw that it was dated for that night.

She didn't understand why her mother was showing her this until she saw the name of the host. It was her friend Amber. More like a friend of the family, actually. Hannah, Hunter, and Amber spent plenty of time together as children. They went to the same schools and hung out in the same groups. Amber's parents were really close with Hannah's, and Amber was like the sister she never had.

Amber moved away a couple of years before Hunter died. For the most part the two of them stayed in touch. They would message each other on Facebook a couple times a week and would Skype each other at least once a month. But after he died, the two of them stopped talking. It was easier to let their friendship fade away than to keep it going without him.

"She is an event planner now, and she's putting a party together to promote her business," Hannah's mother said.

Hannah read the details of the event.

Join us for a masquerade party on the water! Cocktails and appetizers will be provided. Wear your best mask for a night to remember.

"I'm trying to convince your father to come, but he's being stubborn. If you came, he wouldn't be able to say no."

Hannah hadn't prepared to go out, but she was curious to see what Amber's life had turned out like. They hadn't spoken for so long, she wondered if she had changed at all.

"I'll go, but I'll have to go shopping for a dress. I didn't pack anything that fancy."

Her mother smiled. "That's fine, you have plenty of time to visit the mall. Oh, I'm so glad you're coming! I'll go tell your father."

As her mother disappeared down the stairs, Hannah decided to go to the car and bring in her luggage. She opened the trunk and pulled out her suitcase. Then, she rolled it into the house and made her way into the spare room.

Hannah had half a mind to slip out and go to the mall before her parents came up the stairs, but her mother met her in the hallway before she could decide.

"He's coming up to see you," her mother said. She slipped out into the backyard as if she was making an escape.

"Hey, Hannah," her father said from the top of the basement stairs.

"Hi, Dad," Hannah replied. She went over to give her father a big hug.

"So, I guess we're all going to that thing tonight."

"Yeah, I'm just about to head to the mall to pick up a dress."

"Well . . . Okay. We'll see you soon, then. Don't be late for dinner."

Hannah tried not to be upset about her father's lukewarm welcome. She used to be a daddy's girl, and he had always seemed thrilled to see her. He used to make her feel like the favourite. It made Hunter mad when their father took her on special outings and didn't invite him. Hannah missed those days.

When she arrived at the shopping mall she found a directory to see if they had any dress stores. She headed to the Chic Boutique first. She knew what she wanted—a long black dress—so it didn't take long to find one she liked. It had a tight, fitted long sleeve top with a loose floating shirt overtop. It looked like something out of a movie. Hannah ended up trying it on since she knew she had a lot of time.

The dress fit perfectly, and it suited her well. She couldn't help but wish Luke were there to see her in it. She decided to stop in at the hair salon since she found the dress so quickly, and they curled her hair in loose ringlets.

Hannah had started heading towards the exit when she remembered she needed a mask. She went to a few stores and finally found a black mask with silver sparkles around the edges. It tied up with black ribbon in the back. She tried it on, using her phone's camera as a mirror. There was something about the mask that really calmed her. It made her feel like she could be someone else. It made it seem like she could forget everything and just have fun for a night. It covered up her face and all the ways it reminded her of Hunter.

After a simple dinner with her parents, Hannah went to her room to get ready. She took her makeup out of her purse and touched herself up. She put the dress on and threw her clothes on the chair in the corner.

Hannah had brought some black heels, so she didn't have to buy new shoes. She always packed too many pairs of shoes that she usually never needed, but this time they came in handy. She opened up her suitcase and gasped when she saw what was inside.

On top of her clothes sat a postcard. it had a picture of the Black Forest in Germany—the place her parents took her and Hunter when they were twelve. She flipped the postcard over. On the back was something that made Hannah's heart skip a beat. It said, *I miss you.* The handwriting was familiar.

At that moment, Hannah's phone buzzed from inside her purse. She pulled it out and checked the screen to find a message from the same number as before.

I'm so excited to see you.

Hannah threw her phone into her suitcase in a mixture of fear and anger. *Not here*, she thought. *He can't find me here.*

"Hannah, it's time to leave!" her mother yelled.

Hannah zipped up the suitcase and pushed it into the closet.

CHAPTER FORTY-ONE

Luke sat at his kitchen island nursing a beer. Adam was on his way, and Luke was ready. A golf club leaned against the wall near the entryway and around the corner. Every door but the front was locked. He didn't think he'd need it, but he looked up how to quickly call 9-1-1 on his cell phone. He could do it even with his phone in his pocket.

This ends tonight, Luke thought. He rolled the bottom edge of his beer bottle against the stone countertop.

Soon enough, the doorbell rang. Luke got up and checked through the peephole of the solid wood door. There stood Adam, holding a six-pack of locally brewed beer.

Luke opened the door.

"Hey, man!" Adam said. "Good to see you again."

Luke nodded, his face stony. "Come in."

Luke walked down the entryway, careful not to leave his back completely turned, as Adam closed the door behind him and kicked off his shoes. By the time Adam looked up again, Luke had the golf club raised in his hands. Adam backed up against the door.

"Jesus Christ, man!" The beer bottles clanked against one another as the box collided with the door.

"Tell me everything," Luke demanded.

"Yeah. Everything. Of course. Just . . . put that down—please." Adam slowly lowered the case of beer to the floor in front of him. "No hard feelings. We can talk as friends."

Luke gritted his teeth and strengthened his grip on the golf club. "Friends? What the hell sort of friendship has all this been?"

"All what?" Adam's face suddenly shifted. "No, no. Okay, look. Let's just sit down calmly. I know what you've been dealing with, but it wasn't me. I'd be mad too—but it wasn't me."

Luke stared at Adam, trying to judge him. After a few moments, he took a deep breath. "We'll sit. But you're going to have to convince me to put this down."

"Sure. Yeah. Just lead the way." Adam picked the beer up again. Luke led him to the kitchen island and pulled out the nearest chair. Then, he sat himself on the farthest one, laying the golf club in front of him.

"Talk," he said.

"Yeah, okay. So, I don't know if she told you this, but Hannah and I used to have a thing. A few weeks. We'd known each other for a long time, and—"

Luke scowled. He gripped the golf club again.

Adam held his hands in front of him, eyes wide. "But it ended. Completely. One hundred percent." He lowered his hands and paused for a few moments. "After I started seeing her, I started getting threats. Like, weird messages. In my own home. With the doors locked."

Luke relaxed his grip and let his shoulders drop. *I've been such an asshole.*

"I thought so," Adam said. "You've been getting the same threats, haven't you?" He pulled a beer from the case, twisted it open, then slid it to Luke.

"Yeah. And I thought it was you."

"No kidding? I thought you were about to brain me with a golf club because these aren't your brand." Adam grinned weakly as

146

he opened a beer for himself.

"Sorry about that."

"It's okay. I mean, I almost pissed myself, but it's okay. Hannah wouldn't be with you if you weren't a good guy. She doesn't pick bad ones."

Luke smirked at Adam's implied meaning. His heart rate was finally beginning to slow, and the tension faded. "So what happened?"

"About the threats? I listened. I backed off from Hannah. I know—coward. But that shit really got to me. I dunno, I just—I just panicked."

Luke nodded at this. He had never considered backing away, but he knew it might be tempting. To some, anyway.

He took a sip of beer and cleared his throat. "What do you know about this guy? Anything?"

Adam shrugged. "Nothing, really. I wasn't even sure it was a *guy*, so you might already know more than me." He took a sip of his own beer. "I did think for a bit that it might have been Hannah's brother, but he wouldn't have done anything like that. Maybe as a joke, but this wasn't a joke. And, well . . . You know he's dead now, right?"

"I do. So it obviously isn't him."

Adam nodded grimly. Then, after a few moments, he spoke again. "Does Hannah know?"

Luke shook his head. "Didn't want to scare her. And she's . . . She's had worries of her own."

"Maybe she *should* know. I dunno, just—it's a big secret to keep." Adam finished his beer and put the empty bottle in the case. "Just something to think about." He stood and pushed the case towards Luke. "You can keep these. Token of friendship."

"Thanks. And sorry again."

"No worries. See you again, alright?"

"Yeah. See you, Adam."

Luke remained on the bar stool as Adam let himself out. *It is a big secret*, he thought, *and it's not the only one.*

Chapter Forty-Two

Luke fiddled with his phone for a good ten minutes. Adam was right. He was keeping too much from her. He could protect her as well as he could, but it wasn't his place to decide what she shouldn't know.

Something dawned on him, and he started to panic. Luke thought Hannah had flown off to safety. He was going to take care of their problem, and when she returned, the threat would be gone. But Adam wasn't the threat.

Luke needed to know she was still okay. He pulled up Hannah's phone number and tried to call, but the phone just rang until her voice mail picked up. Then, he tried texting her. Luke sat and waited for her reply, but none came.

Maybe she's just busy, he thought. But the longer he waited, the more he worried. What if she was in trouble? It would kill Luke to learn he could have helped her but didn't.

Luke wasn't about to wait for bad news. He called Adam to ask if he knew her parents' address. Luckily, he did.

All Luke had to do was get to the airport and get on the next available flight—whatever the cost.

* * *

Her dad drove while her mother fidgeted with the radio, finally settling on a country station. Hannah sat and looked out the window. Her mind was preoccupied with the postcard. It made her sick to her stomach that the person messing with her knew so much about her life—all the little details. He knew about the gifts her brother had given her for her birthday. He knew where she lived. Unless the text message was a freak coincidence, he knew where her *parents* lived. He knew her family had travelled to the Black Forest when she was younger. She started to suspect people she hadn't seen or heard from in years. She really couldn't trust anyone anymore. Anyone except Luke, and she had left him behind.

Hannah's thoughts shifted to the journal. What had been on those missing pages? What had she lost her chance to learn? The answers were under her nose for months, and she had just let them slip away.

Her father turned into the large parking lot by the bay and drove straight past the valet. The lot was sparsely populated, but he pulled into the farthest stall from the water. Hannah's mother complained about walking the whole way in heels, but he couldn't be swayed.

When the three reached the ramp to the small, docked cruise ship, Hannah's father stopped. "You two go on ahead. I'm going to get a little more air."

Hannah and her mother were handed cocktails as soon as they walked through the doors. The deck of the ship was done up beautifully. Large black curtains surrounded all the corners, and gold-and-silver-sequined tablecloths covered the tables. The sliding glass roof was raised, but it still allowed a wide view of the evening sky. Hannah couldn't help but look up for a few minutes as she tried to see the stars.

Everyone was dressed up and having a good time. She scanned the deck to appreciate all the details Amber had put into the party. The waiters and waitresses wore masks with beautiful matching gowns and tuxedos. The food was themed perfectly to the décor.

Someone came and offered Hannah a cupcake with a mask on it. Amber knew her business.

Small chandeliers hanging from the glass roof trembled with the bass of the loud dance music. Hannah wondered if her mother would approve, but she seemed to be enjoying herself. Her father had also come up to the deck, and Hannah caught him gazing at the sky like she had. There was a bit of old Dad in there after all.

Hannah went to stand by her father. When he noticed her, he gave her half a smile. "This isn't so bad," he said. "I'm glad you came to visit, Hannah bear."

Hannah was surprised by this. It was the warmest he'd been towards her in a year.

"Me too, Dad."

Someone tapped Hannah on the shoulder. Hannah turned around and smiled when she realized who it was. She gave Amber a hug.

"Oh my gosh, you look amazing!" Hannah said. "Your hair is so long now!" *And she's lost weight too*, she thought.

Amber smiled as she tucked one side of her long red hair behind her ear. *Ariel*, Hannah used to call her, after the Disney character. Now she was all grown up. Even in the year that had passed since Hannah last saw her, Amber seemed to have changed.

"I can't believe all this. Did you put everything together yourself?"

"Well, most of it," Amber said. "But I really owe your dad for his help."

My dad? Hannah looked to her father, who had gone and found a place to sit.

"You should come meet some of my friends," Amber said.

Hannah followed, looking back to her father once more.

Amber led Hannah to a group of people near the bar. She couldn't see their whole faces behind their masks, but she could tell they were all very attractive people. The women had their hair curled perfectly and must have had their makeup professionally done. The men wore black suits, each with a different mask.

Amber introduced Hannah to everyone and then signalled for a waitress to come over. She whispered something in the waitress's ear, smirking a little. Hannah wasn't sure what Amber was up to, but she had known her friend to stir up trouble when they were young.

The waitress returned soon after with a tray of shots. Everyone got one, including Hannah. Amber lifted her shot in the air and smiled.

"To good friends and a great night!" she said. Everyone raised their glasses.

Hannah couldn't help but notice a wink from the gentleman across from her. He was strikingly handsome. His name was Jacob—the only name from the round of introductions she could remember.

Hannah felt a little tipsy after the shot. She ordered a milder drink to take with her, and Amber begged her to join the group on the dance floor.

The group made its way onto the dance floor as the DJ shifted to a slower track, and Jacob asked Hannah to dance. She accepted his invitation and followed him into the crowd. He put his arms around her waist and she put her free hand on his shoulder. He looked down at her and smiled.

Halfway through the song, Hannah found herself pushed into Jacob by the movement of the tight crowd. Their eyes met, and she suddenly felt uncomfortable being so close to him. She thought about how much she missed Luke. Hannah pulled away. Once the song was over, he kissed her hand and offered to go get her another drink.

Hannah needed to hear from Luke. *Maybe he texted me*, she thought as she dug through her purse. But her phone wasn't there. *Right. It's in my suitcase.*

"You look nice in that black dress," said a voice from over her shoulder. She felt a pair of hands grab her waist as the man behind her started dancing with her. She tried to pull away.

"Hannah, I told you to stay away from the man with the green eyes," he whispered.

She wrenched herself from him and spun around. This man seemed so familiar. His shape, his eyes—she couldn't see his whole face behind the mask, but she didn't need to. She raised a hand to cover her mouth.

"Hunter?" she said.

The man's eyes flashed, then he frowned. He quickly turned and wove through the crowd. Hannah ran after him, trying not lose him.

Hannah's mind was racing. She was so desperate for the man to be her brother that she ignored how impossible that was. But soon, she lost track of his movement among the flood of suits, dresses, and masks. She stopped.

She had lost him.

Chapter Forty-Three

Hannah woke up the next morning to the sounds of someone making breakfast. She could smell bacon cooking, and it made her stomach growl. She remembered back to when she was young. Her parents would always make breakfast together on the weekends. Her father made pancakes shaped like Mickey Mouse and her mother tried to make eggs shaped as snowmen. They usually didn't turn out very well, but Hannah and her brother would always laugh together at her mother's attempts to crack the second egg directly over the first to make the head.

Hannah thought about the night before as she lowered herself out of bed. She had seen him again—she knew it. But if her brother really was alive, why had nobody else seen him? Why hadn't anyone said anything?

Nobody but Nicole, that is. Maybe Hannah wasn't going crazy after all.

Hannah wished so badly that she could talk to him. She hated living in this world without him. She missed her best friend.

Hannah went over to the closet to grab her suitcase and fish out some clothes. Her phone was still sitting at the top of the bag. She had forgotten to charge it, and now it was dead. She plugged it into an outlet by the bed and got dressed.

By the time she finished brushing the tangles out of her hair, her phone had enough power to turn on. She sat on the edge of the bed and checked her messages. One missed call and two text messages—all from Luke.

Call me back when you can.

Then, twenty minutes after the first:

I'm worried about you, Hannah. Are you ok?

Hannah needed to call him back and tell him everything was fine. Mostly fine, anyway.

She blew past her mother in the kitchen and went out on the deck to make the call. Straight to voicemail. She tried again.

Her mother waved at her from behind the kitchen window. Hannah smiled back.

She had to settle for a text message. *I'm ok. I miss you.*

Hannah returned inside as her mother was setting the table. "Have a seat! Your father should be out of the shower soon."

Hannah checked the serving plates. Bacon, hash browns, buttered toast, and eggs. No cartoon mice or lopsided snowmen. And, of course, only three place settings.

Breakfast went as expected. Hannah's mother held a one-sided conversation while Hannah and her father worked away at their plates. Hannah wanted to bring up what Amber had said the night before—about her father's help—but her mother kept going on until the food was gone and the dishes were cleared away.

"Well, your father and I have to go run some errands in town. We'll be back just before dinner time. Will you be alright on your own today? There's an extra set of keys by the door if you decide to go out."

"Yeah, I'll be fine," Hannah replied.

Her mother smiled and then followed Hannah's father out of the house. Hannah was alone again.

Hannah spent the next few hours wandering the house. Wherever she went, her phone and Hunter's journal kept her company.

She bounced between the patio, the living room, the kitchen, and the spare bedroom she was staying in. None of these places felt comfortable. Nothing on TV could hold her attention. She kept checking her phone for new messages. She kept thinking of Hunter.

She wanted to believe he was alive—that she hadn't imagined seeing him over and over. But if he was, what about the body? And why was he only showing himself now? Was he still hiding from his stalker?

As she aimlessly opened the fridge for the fourth time, Hannah decided this line of thought wasn't getting her anywhere—and it probably wasn't healthy. If Hunter really was alive, she'd know in time.

Still, Hannah couldn't help herself. She thought back to that night again. She thought about that familiar masked figure.

Hannah remembered something else. Amber had mentioned she owed Hannah's father for his help. But for what? What did her father have to do with event planning? The only business she had ever known him to involve himself with was fishing boat rentals, and he had left that business behind. He certainly didn't seem to be in any state to take on new ventures.

Amber's party *had* been on a boat, but it was a decommissioned cruise ship, not a fishing boat.

Hannah had a thought. It bothered her, but she had to investigate.

She walked into her father's home office and started looking through the shelves and drawers. A layer of dust covered everything, and most of the desk drawers were practically empty. But in one of the drawers, next to an old photo album, was a key to the filing cabinet.

Hannah unlocked the filing cabinet and brushed through the files with her fingers, scanning, looking for something that would catch her attention. Something that could help her get closer to the truth.

It wasn't something she noticed right away. She almost missed it. She had closed the drawer, but she opened it up again; something in her gut told her that in the folder labelled *H.A.C.* she would find what she was looking for.

She pulled the file out from the cabinet and fanned the documents across the floor. The paper from the front of the file was a bill of sale for a watercraft. Steven Melbrook to Amber Young. Twenty dollars.

Hannah pulled out her phone to run a search for the make and model listed on the bill of sale. *That explains that*, she thought.

The next page after the bill of sale was a certificate of dissolution. She skimmed through the remaining documents. Business licence, tax papers, service contracts, permits—all bearing the name *Heavy Anchors Co.*

Tucked between a couple of pages, she found something odd: a picture of Hunter from when he was young. He must have been no older than four. It seemed so out of place, but not knowing where it really belonged, Hannah left it where it was.

She sat and looked through every document over and over. She had almost memorized the service contract after reading it so many times. She tried think of why her father would have kept this a secret. And why had he started the business in the first place? His rental company always did well. None of it seemed necessary.

But one piece of information seemed more important than anything else. The boat Hunter was meant to meet someone on the night he died had belonged to her father.

The doorbell rang, and Hannah sat frozen. She didn't want to answer. It rang again, which was followed by several knocks on the door. Hannah stuffed the papers back in the file folder and jammed it into the filing cabinet, locking it and returning the key to the drawer. She then made her way to the front door.

She knew it when saw his outline through the frosted glass.

It was the man with the green eyes.

CHAPTER FORTY-FOUR

When Hannah finally answered the door, Luke felt a wave of relief. He was exhausted, having stayed overnight at the airport while he waited on standby, and he felt it even more as his anxiety faded away. He hugged Hannah tightly and kissed her lips.

"I can't believe you're here," she said, holding both of his hands.

"I needed to see you." Luke tried to sound calm. He didn't want to reveal how much he had panicked when she didn't answer his call or his texts.

Hannah invited Luke inside and led him to the couch. They sat next to one another with their thighs touching. Luke missed the feeling of her body on his.

"Well," she said, "I'm glad you're here. I've had a rough day."

Luke listened as Hannah told him about the evening before. She told him about a postcard she found in her luggage, then she told him about the man she thought was her brother.

"Your brother? Are you sure?" Luke asked.

"No, he was wearing a mask like everyone else, but . . . he knew my name. And it's not the first time I've seen him."

Luke leaned in and studied her face.

"The first time, I thought it was a dream. Then I saw him again at the beach. Last night was the third time. You think I'm going crazy, don't you?"

Luke put his hand on Hannah's knee. "No, I don't think you're crazy." *I'd probably start seeing him everywhere too.*

"That's not all," Hannah said. "I was just in my dad's office, and I found something. My dad had a cruise business he hadn't told me about, and he closed it right after Hunter died."

Luke knit his eyebrows. Once he was sure that was all she had to say, he said, "Okay. That's odd, but what does that have to do with your brother?"

Hannah started toying with her necklace. "His journal. I've been reading it. That's how I found out about his stalker."

"You mean he hadn't told you about it?"

"No. I didn't find out until this month. Anyways, in the journal he said he was supposed to meet someone on a cruise ship. He was supposed to meet them the night he died."

Nobody tells her anything, do they? Luke thought. He shifted his weight as if his guilt had become heavier.

Hannah continued. "I have a feeling my dad knows something about my brother's death that he isn't telling me. But how do you bring *that* up?"

Luke shrugged. "It's not an easy one. But you have a chance now that you're here."

The two sat for a while. Luke wanted to come clean about what he knew, but sitting next to Hannah sapped his resolve.

"Come on," Hannah said. "I'll show you around."

Hannah gave Luke a tour of the house. He noticed there wasn't much in the realm of decorations or personal touches. No family photos, either. Hunter's death must have hit Hannah's parents hard. He made a mental note to avoid the subject around them.

When they got to Hannah's bedroom, Luke dropped down on the bed.

"Wow, you're exhausted, aren't you?" Hannah asked.

"Just a little."

Hannah moved onto the bed next to him. "We can take a rest. I'm pretty tired too. Here." She tugged the covers down, and Luke maneuvered himself to let her. He pressed himself against Hannah's back and put his arm around her as she pulled the covers up.

Luke fell asleep in minutes.

The next thing he knew, Hannah had turned around and was kissing him on the neck. Luke met her lips with his. He wanted her. Soon, her legs were wrapped around his waist.

He heard the front door shut, and they both pulled away. Luke briefly flashed back to high school. This probably wasn't how he wanted to greet Hannah's parents.

Luke and Hannah darted out of the bed, and Hannah made quick work of straightening the blankets. Luke wordlessly followed her down the stairs.

"Oh!" Said the woman who must have been Hannah's mother. "We were wondering who the other car belonged to. And you must be . . ."

"I'm Luke. Pleased to meet you." Luke held his hand out.

"Luke, this is my Mom and Dad."

Hannah's father sized Luke up for a moment, nodded a greeting, then turned towards the kitchen with a bag of groceries.

"So, Luke," began Hannah's mother. "Do you live nearby?"

"Victoria, actually. In the area for business—I just came to visit."

"Oh! So are you two—"

Hannah interrupted. "Yes. We are."

Hannah's mother started a bit at Hannah's abruptness, but she recovered quickly. "Well, you can stay for dinner if you like. It'll be nice to get to know you."

Luke couldn't resist the offer. Now that he was with Hannah, he didn't want to leave her side. With the warmest smile he could muster, he said, "I'd love to."

During dinner, conversation flowed smoothly. Hannah's mother was easy to talk to. In fact, she hardly allowed a single moment of silence. She asked Luke about his work, and Hannah's father even chimed in about the local hockey team.

Luke felt relaxed and at home. He wondered what it would have been like to meet Hannah under normal circumstances. He wondered if Hunter would have welcomed him as warmly, were he still alive. Luke wished he could have met the man.

CHAPTER FORTY-FIVE

After dinner, Hannah and Luke offered to do the dishes. Hannah's parents lingered at the dining table as Hannah led Luke to the kitchen. Hannah spoke in a low voice so her words wouldn't carry.

"That went okay. I think my dad likes you."

"You sure?" Luke said. "He seemed really quiet."

"That was way more than I can usually get out of him. I think he actually smiled once or twice."

"I'll take your word."

Hannah passed Luke the first clean dish to dry. Her hands grazed Luke's, and she glanced towards her parents. She hoped they would soon get up and leave. Hannah wanted to kiss Luke—wanted to take in his scent.

"I really missed you, Hannah. I was scared that something might have happened to you."

"I'm just happy I could see you. Everything that's happened . . ." Hannah wrung out the dishcloth and frowned. "You're staying here tonight, aren't you?"

"If that's okay. I was going to stay with my sister, but if your family doesn't mind—"

"They won't."

Luke brushed Hannah's hair back behind her ears and looked

into her eyes. He pulled her close and kissed her softly. From over Luke's shoulder, Hannah saw the backs of her parents as they left the dining room. *Finally*. She wrapped her arms around Luke and pressed his body against hers.

When they finished the dishes, Hannah and Luke curled up under a blanket and watched a movie. Hannah nodded in and out of sleep in the comfort of Luke's presence.

Later, she woke up to the sound of a woman singing. The lights and TV were off, and Luke slept soundly at the other side of the couch. She quietly got up, trying not to wake him.

She could hear the sound coming from somewhere in the house. It was a song she recognized. Her mother used to sing it to put her and Hunter asleep when they were little.

As she followed the voice, she noticed a dim light shining from the crack underneath the spare bedroom door. She could now tell it was her mother's voice. It sounded younger, but it was hers. Hannah remembered the times as a child when she would get homesick during sleepovers. She would call her mom, who would sing that song to her.

Hannah slowly turned the door handle and entered the bedroom. Her laptop was open on the bed. An old home video played on the screen: Hannah's mother singing to a young Hunter—no older than a year and a half.

Hannah couldn't bear to watch. She closed the lid, silencing the singing and hiding the image of her brother. She wanted so badly to see him again, but not like this.

Hannah rolled onto the bed and stared at the ceiling. How did that video get on her laptop? If it was her parents, why would they do that? If it was someone else . . .

Eventually, she fell asleep.

* * *

Hannah could feel the dry dirt underneath her fingernails. She had blood on her ripped clothes. She walked towards the water holding his hand. It was time for her to let him go. She knew her brother had to die. She knew that things would never be the same.

As they walked closer to the water, she stopped. His fingers slowly detached from hers as his feet touched the water. He went in past his knees and kept going further and further until only his head and shoulders were exposed. He looked back at her as she cried.

He opened his mouth and said, "Look harder, Hannah."

And with that, he let the water take him home.

Hannah awoke before the sun was up. She knew her dreams were trying to tell her something important. She could feel it. She grabbed the laptop and played the video again.

This time, she paid close attention. She recognized the room. It was the same room she and Hunter had shared for years, but something was odd. There was only one crib.

Hannah's mother finished her song and leaned in to kiss her child on the forehead. She smiled then said, "Good night, Aidan."

Chapter Forty-Six

Not Hunter. *Aidan.*

What is this? Hannah thought. She pinched herself. *No, this is real. But isn't that Hunter?*

Aidan. Aidan. The name sounded familiar, but Hannah couldn't place it.

As she scoured her brain, an old memory surfaced.

Let me out! I can't see!

No, the voice on the other side of the door had said, *you're a prisoner. You're staying in there until we get to shore.*

I'm telling mom! Hannah had tried to wrench the doorknob and free herself, but he was stronger than her. She screamed and slammed her small fists against the closet door. *I hate you, Aidan!*

Hannah remembered a face. He had looked like Hunter, but he was bigger—older.

Aidan. Aidan.

Hannah closed the laptop again and went to the bookshelf where her parents kept their photo albums. She flipped through each one, but she only found the same old photos she knew.

Then, she remembered what she had found the day before.

She put the albums back on the shelf and went to the home office. In the drawer where she had found the key was another photo album, and inside the album were more photos of Hannah's family. But each of these photos had something the others didn't: a third child.

Hannah turned to the most recent photograph—a family photo from when Hannah was three or four. The third child was taller than Hunter, and he had only one dimple where Hunter had two. Otherwise, the resemblance was uncanny.

She grabbed the key from the drawer and unlocked the file cabinet, digging out the photo she had stumbled across before. This time, she examined it closely, comparing it to the images in the photo album. The differences were hard to spot, but she knew that photo wasn't of Hunter after all. It was Aidan.

*　*　*

Luke awoke to Hannah shaking his shoulder. It felt like he hadn't slept more than a few hours. Before he could shake the sleep off, Hannah grabbed him and led him outside. The sun hadn't come up yet.

Hannah sat him down on a patio chair and stood in front of him. "Luke. I think I know who's been doing this to me."

Luke waited for her to continue.

"You know how I said I've been seeing my brother? Well, I think I really did."

"But isn't he—"

"A *second* brother."

Luke ran a hand through his hair. "You have two brothers?"

"I don't remember much about him—I'd forgotten completely until now—but I think he went away when we were little." Hannah shook her head. "I don't know why, but I think he's the one who did it. The one who did everything."

"Because he looks like Hunter?"

"Not just that, but . . ." Hannah's eyes flashed, then she levelled them at Luke. "I don't remember telling you his name."

165

I guess it's time, Luke thought. *I have to tell her.*

"Look, Hannah, I'm sorry for not telling you sooner, but I was the one who found Hunter on the beach. I called the police."

Luke could see the disbelief forming on Hannah's face. "Why didn't you—"

He was wide awake now, and the words just poured out. "There's more. I saw another man that night. At the beach. I think he killed Hunter. And since I started seeing you, someone's been breaking into my house and leaving threats—and you said someone was messing with you, too—and he left me a page of Hunter's journal. When you said you had it, I knew he had been close to you. And I thought it was Adam, but it wasn't, and when you didn't answer, I thought you were in trouble." When he finished, he realized he wasn't looking at Hannah anymore. He was ashamed to.

"Why didn't you tell the police you saw someone that night?"

Luke could hear it in her voice, but he had to look. He saw tears rolling down Hannah's cheeks. She held her chest as if she had been stabbed.

Luke started to stand—he needed to comfort her—but Hannah held a hand out to stop him.

Hannah's voice trembled with anger. "Why didn't you tell *me*?" Her words ripped through him like waves crashing through water.

"I—I didn't want to worry you."

"So *you* could protect me? How can I trust you if you don't trust me?"

Luke didn't know what to say. He had hoped she would understand. There had to be something he could tell her to make her feel better.

"Go," Hannah said.

"Hannah, I love—"

"Get out. Now."

Luke nodded solemnly. He stood up, walked to the backyard gate, and let himself out. Before he closed the gate behind him, he looked back at Hannah one last time. Her back was turned.

Luke got in his car and drove down the street, parking only a block away. He knew he couldn't leave her again. No matter how angry she was, he had to be there for her. He knew she was in trouble. He needed to be there for when her brother came for her.

PART FOUR

CHAPTER FORTY-SEVEN

Luke sat parked near Hannah's parents' house, weighing his options. Even if Hannah didn't want to see him, he knew she would need him. If she could never forgive him? Well, that was her choice. At least he could keep her safe.

But he couldn't stay parked there forever. Hannah hadn't planned to return to Victoria until the next day, and he was ill equipped for a stakeout. He considered visiting his sister and asking to stay the night, but he didn't need the distraction of family.

No, Luke needed to be in Victoria. If Hannah beat him there, he would be unable to keep an eye on her until he managed to get a flight. He could be waiting in standby for days. Who knows what could happen in that time?

On the way to the airport, Luke started thinking about his apology to Hannah. It would have to be good.

*   *   *

Hannah didn't know what was worse: her anger or her sorrow. She sat in her parents' living room, sipping on a bottle of beer, and wondered where Luke had gone. Part of her wished she didn't care—that she could just forget about him and how he betrayed her trust. The truth was, she was still consumed by thoughts of him. How could he have gone that whole time without telling her he was there the night Hunter died? How could he hide that he was also being followed—that his home had been no safer than hers? Hannah felt waves of nausea as the thoughts rolled around in her head.

She sat in the silent room and tried to wipe her thoughts out of her mind. She turned to her phone for a distraction, tapping through her text messages. There were a couple from Adam. She opened them up and read.

Hey, Hannah. I hope you don't mind, but I met with Luke. He seems like a good guy.

I hope everything is alright. I heard you went to see your parents. I just want you to know that if there's anything you need, I'm here for you.

This sudden warmness from Adam surprised her. He hadn't given her that sort of attention for a long time. Why had he met with Luke? Was Adam still looking out for her, even after what had happened between them?

Hannah remembered the skiing trip about a year and a half before. Hunter and Adam went every year, but that year they had invited Hannah. Hunter, outgoing guy that he was, made friends with a group of Australian tourists—which left Adam and Hannah alone. When the lifts closed, they went back to the hotel where they had connecting rooms. Hannah unlocked the door between their suites and invited Adam over. The two of them indulged in the minibar, each having a few shots and a couple of beers.

They were exhausted from skiing, so they decided to stay in and order room service for dinner. It was calm and casual. Hannah didn't feel pressured when she was with Adam. He was charming and kind. As it grew darker outside, the two of them decided to watch a movie. Adam insisted on sitting on the couch next to the bed, but Hannah made him stay next to her. As the movie went on, they moved closer and closer to one another. Eventually, her head was on his chest and his fingers were interlaced with her own.

They didn't sleep together that night; that didn't happen until two weeks later. Hunter had been working a night shift, so Hannah had the house to herself. Adam came over with dinner and a bottle of rum. They started watching another movie, but they barely made it past the opening act.

The next morning, Adam snuck out when Hunter was fast asleep in his room.

Then, there was nothing. Adam stopped returning Hannah's calls, and he wouldn't even spend the evening with Hunter if Hannah was around. The whole thing was confusing, frustrating, and painful.

Hannah wondered if Adam had been thinking of her all along since then. He hadn't dated anyone that she knew about—and she would have known. Tawn didn't know about her former relationship with Adam, but otherwise, relationships weren't things you could keep quiet around her.

CHAPTER FORTY-EIGHT

The sun was starting to set. Hannah's parents had left that morning, and they still weren't back yet. As Hannah reheated leftovers from the night before, she wondered if her parents were avoiding her. She ate alone, wondering how she would bring up the subject of her estranged and forgotten brother.

Hannah felt lost. She wished Luke was still there with her. Several times, she stopped herself from texting him. She would remind herself what he had kept from her. He had looked her in the eyes so many times and never said a word about it. Still, a part of her felt comforted by thoughts of Luke, and she couldn't deny it. He was like air to her—the only thing that made her feel like she could see and think clearly.

Hannah went to the bathroom and started getting ready for bed. She brushed her teeth and splashed cold water on her face. She walked back to her room and got underneath the covers, feeling utterly alone.

Hannah lay on her back, staring at the ceiling. Thoughts kept coming to her mind, and she could not push them out. She wanted more than anything to feel normal—to have a night where she didn't go to sleep scared or upset.

She realized how much she had taken her life for granted before all of this. She had everything she could ever want, and most of all she had Hunter. He was her other half. Without him, she didn't know who she was anymore. Everything was different. Her parents were still around, but they too were different. Nothing or no one would ever be the same.

Hannah woke up several times throughout the night. Each time she would be soaked in sweat or freezing from kicking the blankets off. She couldn't get thoughts of Luke, Aidan, and Hunter out of her mind.

She wondered how Aidan could do this to them—to his own family. She tried to pull memories out of her mind from when they were young, but there wasn't much there. She wondered why he was absent from so many of her childhood memories. She wondered if she was crazy—if any of this had been real. Hannah tried in vain to sort out which of her memories were real and which were created by her dreams.

She wished it were morning.

*   *   *

Hannah heard her mother calling her name. She opened her eyes and rubbed them with her hands. She was surprised she managed to get any sleep. Hannah put on a clean t-shirt and jean shorts and walked into the kitchen. Her mother was making lunch. As soon as she saw the food, she realized she had no appetite.

Hannah leaned against the counter and listened to her mother tell her about their night playing board games at a friend's house. It seemed almost alien to Hannah, imagining her parents playing board games. They had never done anything like that in Victoria. She had a hard time seeing them as the same people as before.

Hannah didn't need to be at the airport for a few hours, so she decided to spend some time sitting outside on the deck with her parents. She could pack later.

Her mother brought the tray of sandwiches outside and set it on the glass table. To humour her mother, Hannah took a sandwich and nibbled at it. She felt ill at ease, and the heat radiating off the deck and collecting in the patio furniture made her sweat. She sipped a glass of lemonade with ice, but it did little to ease the heat.

She felt the questions rising in her throat and knew she had to get them out while she had the chance. If she asked her parents in person, she would at least be able to see their reactions.

"Why haven't you said anything about Hunter? He died a year ago yesterday. Don't tell me you forgot."

Silence.

The next question came out before Hannah could think.

"Who's Aidan?"

Hannah looked at each of her parents to try to read their faces. Both of them registered shock. Hannah had taken them completely off guard, and there was no hiding it. She waited as they composed themselves. She wasn't going to let them dodge her question. She needed answers, and she knew they would have them.

Hannah's mother was the first to speak. Her father sat in silence, seemingly glad to let his wife take the burden. He wouldn't look Hannah in the eyes.

"When did you start to remember?" Hannah's mother said.

"Just answer me, please."

"Aidan was our first child." Her mother spoke tentatively, loss and regret clear in her face and posture.

"So I did have another brother. Why do I barely remember him?" Hannah asked. She had so many questions; she wished her mother would speak faster.

"I don't know, Hannah, but . . . Do you remember when you were six and you caught some frogs when we spent the day at the park?"

Of course she did. It had happened a long time ago, but it was one of her few unpleasant memories of Hunter. Hannah had caught several frogs and gathered them in a bucket. She wanted to keep them as pets, so when she got home, she set about making a proper home for them. She found a large plastic bin, poked holes in the lid, and gathered rocks and twigs to decorate the improvised aquarium. After she filled the bottom of the bin with water, she moved the frogs from the bucket and went to gather insects to feed to the frogs.

When she returned, she found Hunter standing over the frogs with a large rock in his hand. The frogs that were scattered around his feet didn't move—they were all crushed. Hannah cried and ran to her parents.

Whenever Hannah brought up this memory, Hunter would deny it. He'd say he wasn't with them that day—but of course he was.

"What does that have to do with Aidan?" Hannah replied.

Hannah's mother sighed. "Hunter was right, Hannah. It wasn't him who killed your frogs—of course he'd never do such a thing, poor Hunter. It was Aidan"

"We left it alone because . . ." added her father, who stared into space as he searched for the words. "Well, we thought it was better for you to wrongly accuse Hunter than to remember Aidan. Better for both of you."

"How in the hell could that be better?" Hannah asked. A glob of egg salad hit her leg, and she put her partially-crushed sandwich back on the tray.

Hannah's mother wiped tears from her face and rushed inside, closing the patio door behind her.

Hannah's father looked at her. She couldn't tell if he was angry or not. Was he upset that she had opened up Pandora's box? Was he upset that his secrets were about to come to the forefront? Perhaps her mother hadn't known about his little side business. There were too many unknowns, and Hannah wanted answers. She wanted the truth. She was tired of the secrets. She wanted to know more about her other brother—the brother who took away her best friend.

"Hannah, it's complicated." Her father's response was vague and cold.

"I don't care, Dad! I have the right to know." Hannah felt her temper continue to rise.

Her dad sat back in his chair and exhaled loudly.

"Hannah, Aidan had some issues. We weren't able to control him, and your mother and I had to make a difficult decision when he was young." Hannah could sense some shakiness in her father's voice.

She waited for him to continue. The silence rippled between them. She couldn't wait any longer.

"What happened? What made you send him away? What was the final straw?" Hannah hardly recognized her own voice.

Her father's face grew sombre. She could see that he remembered vividly.

"It was a lot of things, but . . . Do you remember the day at the beach?"

Hannah shook her head and focused on her father.

"That was when we knew we had to do something. That was when he tried to drown your brother." His voice faltered, and he couldn't stop staring at his lap and rubbing his thumb over the back of his hand.

"We ignored the signs before. We thought it was just typical juvenile behaviour, but the day at the beach, the truth surfaced, and we couldn't put it off it any longer."

Hannah was speechless.

"Your mother and I had to make a difficult decision. One of the hardest decisions we ever made, but we did it for you and you brother. We just wanted you to be safe."

Hannah closed her eyes and saw him. She saw Aidan as a child; the three of them playing together. They were blood. She didn't understand why Aidan would want to hurt them.

"What do you mean you had to make a difficult decision? What happened?" Hannah didn't understand how her parents could have kept this from her all of this time. Aidan was her brother.

"Your father and I took him to see a child psychiatrist." Hannah hadn't even heard her mother come back outside. She sat down next to her father and continued to speak.

"There were so many signs we tried to ignore. He had an unpredictable temper. One moment he would be fine, the next he was smashing dishes and hitting things until his fists bled. And he could be cruel. His first school kicked him out for torturing the class pet. But we didn't think he would ever hurt you or Hunter. He was very protective of you two—you especially."

Hannah watched her mother's face as the tears returned.

Her father finished the story. "When he tried to hurt Hunter at the beach, we knew we didn't have any choice. We had to protect you and Hunter." His tone sounded more like he was trying to convince himself than Hannah.

"You were so upset that day," her mother said. "But a few weeks later, you seemed to have forgotten all about him. Hunter remembered, but we thought—we thought it would be better if you didn't. We sat Hunter down and asked him not to mention Aidan around you. He slipped a few times, but when he did mention Aidan, you didn't seem to know who he was talking about."

Hannah knew that what they were saying was true. Memories started flooding back to her, and she felt sadness take over her anger. It was like a part of her knew all along that it was never just the two of them. There were always three. How had she pushed him so far out of her memories?

"So . . . Where is he now?"

"We don't know," her mother said. "We haven't heard from him since last summer."

"A few months before your brother's passing, your mother and I got a call from Aidan. He had been out of the facility for a while, but he was having trouble finding a stable job. No employment history, so he could never make it to the interview stage."

Hannah felt sympathy for her brother. She wondered how hard it must have been for him to be separated from his family, his brother and sister, and then to struggle so much to find a job. But the sympathy quickly turned back into anger. She wasn't going to forget that he had taken away the most important person to her.

"I decided to help your brother out. A part of me felt guilty for sending him to a facility at such a young age. It felt like your mother and I had failed him—like we could have tried harder to keep him and make sure he was on the right track. There wasn't room for him at the rental company, so I gave him a loan to take some classes—get a trade, maybe. But he blew the money on a car."

The black BMW, Hannah thought.

"Maybe he was manipulating me—trying to force my hand. I don't know. But I still wanted to help. I asked around, and nobody had work for him. Then, I found an opportunity. Someone I knew was selling an almost-new cruise ship. So, I bought it and started a new business for Aidan to work at."

"Heavy Anchors," Hannah said.

Her father didn't look surprised. It was as if he knew Hannah had been looking through his things.

"That's it. But it didn't last long. When Hunter died, I"—he cleared his throat—"I couldn't stand living there anymore. Couldn't stand the water. Still can't. I knew Aidan couldn't run the company without me, so I shut it down—and he went ballistic. Started breaking things and, well, I called the police."

Hannah's father slouched over and tapped his knees with his fingers. He looked over at his wife before he continued. "We didn't know what to do, but I couldn't stay. Aidan ended up going to jail. If he behaved in there, he's out by now, but he hasn't contacted us again. I know this sounds horrible, but I'm glad he hasn't."

Hannah sat with her parents for what felt like an eternity. No one said anything more. She still had questions, but she didn't know where to start. She just wanted to go home. She wanted to be back at her house—back in her own bed. She missed Hunter so much it hurt.

Her mother drove her to the airport later that day. The drive was quiet. Hannah's mother finally broke the silence as she parked at the drop-off point.

"I'm sorry we didn't tell you about Aidan sooner—when you were old enough to handle it again. The psychiatrist recommended it, but we just couldn't." Her mother sounded defeated.

Hannah couldn't speak. She knew that if she said anything she would break down into tears, and that would make her mother feel even worse. Instead, she looked over at her mother and forced a half smile. She grabbed her mother's hand and held it briefly. It wasn't much, but Hannah knew the gesture meant a lot to her mother.

Chapter Forty-Nine

Hannah's phone had been on silent all day. She knew Luke would try to contact her, but she didn't want to hear it. Nothing he had to say could erase what he had done.

When she got through airport security, she checked her phone. Sure enough, there was a message from him waiting. Hannah wanted to just ignore it. She tapped his name despite herself.

Hannah, can we please talk? I'm sorry.

She shook her head to no one in particular. If she did speak with him again, it would be on her own time.

She had more messages: one from Adam and one from Tawn. She checked Tawn's first and learned that Tawn and most of Hannah's friends would be at a party that night. Hannah was invited, if she wanted to go.

She opened the message from Adam next.

Can I see you when you're back in town? We should catch up.

Hannah wasn't sure what had gotten into him. She remembered how things used to be between her and Adam. She missed him. If their relationship could go back to the way it was, would that be so bad? Plus, she had to admit that Adam was handsome and charming. If there was any of her old life she could get back, that was something.

Hannah decided she'd think about it when she got home. Soon, she had boarded the plane. She was exhausted. All her restless nights were catching up to her. For once, she wished she could have more time off work.

Hannah dreamt about Aidan on the plane. She saw him standing across the street from her home. He was wet. She knew where he had been. She walked outside. Thunder roared and shook the pavement, and lightning lit up the sky. Each flash illuminated his face, and she noticed another difference with each glimpse. Hunter had two dimples. He had one. Hunter's teeth were straight—almost perfect. His one front tooth sat higher than the other. His nose was narrower; his jaw, sharper. How had she not seen it sooner?

She walked up to him. He stood, waiting for her to approach.

"Why did you do this to us? To him?"

He looked her in the eyes then tilted his head back. He laughed as he looked up at the sky. She didn't see an ounce of remorse in his eyes. He didn't care. He never had.

Hannah started to walk away, and he grabbed her wrist before she could leave. He pulled her in close and grabbed her by the hair.

"I'm not finished with you yet." His voice was filled with hatred. It made her feel cold inside.

She woke up to turbulence. *Can't I go to sleep just once without dreaming?*

The plane landed shortly after, and she got off and grabbed her suitcase from baggage claim. Now came the part she had been dreading: picking her car up from Luke's. She hoped she could drive it away without incident, but her instinct told her he'd be waiting.

Luckily, her instinct was wrong. As she pulled up to his house in an Uber, she saw only her own car in his driveway. Maybe he hadn't returned from Vancouver yet. Maybe she wouldn't have to see him again.

Hannah got home late in the afternoon. She tried to relax, but her home felt lonely. She found herself really looking forward to going out with Tawn and her other friends. That wouldn't be for hours, though.

She pulled up Adam's message and wrote a reply. *I'm back now. Do you want to get dinner tonight? Just the two of us?*

She was about to add that it was okay if he couldn't make it on such short notice, but Adam's message appeared before she could hit send. *Absolutely! I'll pick you up in about three hours. See you then?*

Hannah had more than enough time to shower and get ready for the evening. As she picked her outfit, she found she was really excited to spend some time alone with Adam again. She checked herself in the mirror, hoping he would like the black over-the-shoulder t-shirt and jean shorts.

Adam texted her around seven o'clock to say he would be there in five minutes. She sat on the couch and checked her phone. There were no new messages. A part of her felt disappointed that Luke didn't message her again—wanted for him to try to fight for her. But she doubted things could ever be the same between them, knowing what she knew. She hoped she could ever get over him.

Hannah's doorbell rang, and she quickly checked herself in the mirror once more before she answered. As the door swung open, Adam smiled a charming smile and handed her some roses.

"Come in! I just need to grab my purse. Be right back." Hannah went to the kitchen to grab a vase for the flowers. As she unwrapped them and transferred them to the vase, she found a note. *I'm sorry for being a jerk. Love, Adam.*

Hannah returned with her purse and gave Adam an appraising look. She couldn't deny that he was handsome. His muscles showed through his dark blue polo shirt and dark grey pants. Her thoughts flashed back to their time together—when things were still normal. She remembered the feeling of his lips on hers. She felt a wave of excitement as she remembered his strong hands against her body. It had been a long time since Hannah saw Adam in that way. She hoped it would last.

Hannah locked the door behind them, and Adam pinched her arm gently. She smiled.

He remembered.

CHAPTER FIFTY

Luke lucked into an early return flight. He didn't even have to wait in standby. The first flight after he had arrived at the airport had plenty of empty seats.

After his plane landed, he called James.

"Hey, buddy," James said. "Back already?"

"Yeah, sort of."

"'Sort of'? Well, are you coming in tomorrow? It's been pretty quiet, but we still have some updates you need to handle."

"I need a little more time. Garrett can handle the updates—I've shown him how. Look, James, I need a favour."

"Garrett, huh? If you say so. What's the favour?"

"I need to swap cars with you for a few days."

"Swap cars? Buddy, I'd be glad to, but I still haven't replaced mine yet. Won't be driving for a few weeks—at least. What do you need to swap for, anyway?"

"Uh . . ." *Shit*, Luke thought. *I should have thought this through.*

"You in trouble or something? I'd be glad to help out or whatever, but if it's a big thing, I need to know what's up."

"Nah, it's nothing. I'll figure something out. Talk to you later, alright?"

"Okay. Just don't say I didn't offer."

Luke hung up and headed to the car rental desk, wondering why that hadn't been his first move. He didn't feel as sharp as usual. Hannah's extreme reaction to his confession caught him off guard, and he found himself reliving that moment in his head.

I'll make this better, he kept thinking. *I'll fix this.*

The early flight allowed Luke to sleep at home this time instead of at the airport. But the next morning, he was back at the airport again. He watched the arrivals area closely whenever a flight from Vancouver was scheduled to land. Hannah hadn't told him when her flight would be coming in, and he didn't want to take any chances.

Hoping Hannah's mood had turned, Luke sent her a quick text apologizing and asking to talk. She didn't respond. He hoped her phone was just turned off for the flight, but he didn't feel very optimistic.

Luke waited for hours. After his second airport meal, he once again turned his attention to arrivals. Another plane had just landed. He watched the crowd filtering through the concourse for any sign of Hannah.

There she is. Luke turned in his seat to hide his face, counting the seconds until she would be safely past and moving towards baggage claim. When he could be sure it was safe, he sped out the door and towards the parking lot.

He moved the blue rental sedan close enough to the exit that he could see everyone leave but far enough that Hannah wouldn't notice him. Then, he waited. Dozens of people passed through the doors while Luke watched. Then, finally, he saw Hannah again.

Hannah noticed his car and started walking towards it. *Oh, no. Oh, no.*

Just as Hannah had gotten uncomfortably close, another blue sedan pulled in front of Luke. It stopped, and Hannah got in. Luke let out his breath.

He followed Hannah to his house, where she moved her luggage into her own car. He scanned his surroundings for a black BMW. If this second brother had returned to Victoria already, it didn't seem like he was following Hannah yet. Luke wondered how long he could keep this up. *Show yourself, you creep.*

When Hannah parked at home, Luke began to feel like a bit of a creep himself. He thought back to her accusation over the phone a week before—back to her vulnerability when he met her on the beach. He pushed the thoughts down. *I'm doing this for her*, he thought. *Once her brother is out of the way, we can be together again.*

Luke watched and waited. As time passed, he flipped between boredom, determination, and self-doubt. He cursed himself for not bringing food.

Around seven o'clock, a car pulled up—but it wasn't the black BMW Luke expected. Adam stepped out of the car with a bouquet of roses. When Hannah opened the door, Luke caught a glimpse of her smile. A pang of jealousy hit him as Adam followed her inside. Luke had to force himself to stay in his car.

This doesn't change anything, Luke thought. *I'm going to keep her safe.*

Chapter Fifty-One

Adam drove a bit faster than Hannah would have liked, but she didn't stop him. If she was going to give him another chance, she had to accept him as he was—not try to turn him into Luke. Adam meant adventure, and maybe that was what Hannah needed.

Whenever her thoughts drifted to Luke, she got an ache in her stomach. She didn't want to think about him anymore, and she hated that she couldn't keep the thoughts away.

Adam looked over and smiled at Hannah as he drove. She smiled back at him and regained her focus. She wanted to give this a try. She wanted to see if they could start again where they had left off. He deserved a chance.

They pulled up to a downtown hotel. "Ever been here before?" Adam said.

Hannah gave him a confused look.

"The restaurant on the top floor is really nice. You'll like it."

"Oh, right," Hannah said. "No, I haven't. But Tawn told me about it."

"She was the one who recommended it to me."

Adam had another advantage there: Hannah's friends already liked him. They hung around the same people.

He opened the car door for her and grabbed her hand. He escorted her through the main lobby and into the elevator, looking very comfortable with the building. Hannah wondered who else he had taken there. She couldn't help but feel a bit jealous. The feeling surprised her.

When they got to the top floor, Adam let Hannah lead the way. She looked around as they were led to their table by the hostess. It was a beautiful evening, and Hannah loved that the restaurant's tall windows let in plenty of natural light. It made her feel safe and comforted. Adam ordered them each a house drink—some kind of martini. Hannah wasn't sure she would like it, but she went with it. Surprisingly, she found it quite good. It was a little strong for her usual taste, but a strong drink suited her just fine at the moment.

Their table overlooked the water, and she noticed all the couples eating around them. It was simple and romantic. Hannah had forgotten what simple felt like. She thought about what life would be like with Adam. Exciting, adventurous—but comfortable. She knew he would do anything for her. Her mind suddenly switched gears to Luke. She tried to shove his image out of her mind.

"Hey," Adam said. He sipped his drink, waiting for Hannah's full attention. "I don't know if you noticed the card, but—"

"I did." Hannah smiled. "It's okay. You must not have wanted to risk your friendship with Hunter."

Adam looked down at his drink.

"He would've been fine with it, you know."

Adam nodded and raised his eyes to her. "I know. I've missed you, Hannah."

The two of them shared a nice dinner together. The food was amazing—some of the best Hannah had ever tried. She was a bit tipsy from all the drinks, and it seemed that Adam was as well. He told her he would leave his car at the restaurant and ordered an Uber to take them to the party. *Adventurous, but smart*, she reminded herself.

He paid the bill, and the two of them went back to the elevator.

When they got inside, something came over Hannah. She wanted to turn back time. As soon as the doors closed, she pushed him up against the elevator door and kissed him. He kissed her back and grabbed her hair with his hands. When the elevator opened, she pulled away. She smiled at him and turned to the lobby. Adam looked up at her with his blue eyes and smiled back.

It was a nice kiss, but it didn't feel the same as it had with Luke. Hannah craved that feeling.

Adam grabbed her hand, and the thought left her as quickly as it came.

CHAPTER FIFTY-TWO

Adam and Hannah kept locking eyes on the ride over. Adam's legs were pressed against her thigh, and she didn't want to move away. She just wanted a night where she could forget everything that had happened to her. She wanted to be free of all her pain and all the drama. She wanted things to be normal . . . even if she knew it wouldn't last.

When they got to the party, Adam grabbed Hannah's hand and led her inside, past the crowd of people near the doorway. The pictures on the wall vibrated from the bass of the loud dance music. In the kitchen, Adam grabbed drinks for Hannah and himself.

Hannah looked around. She didn't recognize anyone. She wanted to ask Adam if they were at the right party, but she didn't feel like shouting. Either way, she was determined to have a good time.

Soon, Tawn found them. "Hannah!" she yelled, going in for a hug. When she stepped back, she gestured to Adam with her eyes and gave Hannah a questioning look. Hannah just smiled and shrugged.

Tawn gestured for the two of them to follow her. They stepped outside after her, and Hannah saw her friends sitting around a fire pit. That was more like it. She missed the days when she would go to parties and drink without a care in the world, and her friends completed the picture.

Hannah and her friends sat and talked around the fire. They did a couple of tequila shots, which Hannah knew she would regret in the morning. She kept noticing Adam staring at her out of the corner of her eye. Eventually, she gave in and started making eye contact. If her friends knew, so what? She smiled as they held each other's attention. She got up and went to go get another drink, knowing that Adam would follow her. She liked the attention.

Hannah noticed her steps were scattered as she walked into the kitchen. She had planned on getting drunk, but she didn't expect it would hit her so hard. Adam came up behind Hannah and grabbed her waist to steady her. She turned, held on to his arms, and raised her head. She kissed him on the lips. All she could think about when she kissed him was Luke. She wished it was him holding her.

Hannah pulled away and went to the bathroom. She washed her hands and tried to steady herself in the mirror. Her body was swaying from the liquor. She wished she hadn't had so much to drink. She hated the feeling of losing control.

Hannah left the bathroom and made her way down the hallway. Everything was off. It felt like the house was spinning. The walls looked blurry.

She saw his face, and the spinning stopped. The last thing she could remember was her worst nightmare standing in front of her, and there was nothing she could do about it.

Chapter Fifty-Three

Luke sat in his rental car at the end of the street, watching people go in and out of a house party. He hadn't expected Hannah to go to a party the same day her flight returned from Vancouver—it seemed so unlike the Hannah he knew. Still, it was less tedious than guarding her home.

And at least she and Adam weren't alone anymore.

Luke could hear the music from where he sat. He wondered if there would be any noise complaints. It was a weekday after all, and it was getting late.

As Luke watched the house, he heard a familiar roar. He turned towards the sound. It came from the alleyway behind the houses, and it was approaching the end of the street where he had parked. Moments later, he saw a black BMW burst from the alleyway and speed down the street, passing right behind where Luke had parked.

That's no coincidence.

Luke started the car and screeched onto the main road. He recognized the familiar taillights a couple of blocks ahead. His blood pumped hard with fear and adrenaline. Careful to keep his eyes on the road, Luke held the voice-activation button on his phone. He needed to know if Hannah was in that car.

"Call Adam."

The phone rang twice as Luke sped up to beat a yellow light.

"Luke?" Adam shouted from the other end. Luke could hear voices and muffled music in the background. Adam must have been outside.

"Adam. This is very important. Is Hannah with you?"

"Uh . . . Look, man. Hannah, she—she asked to come out. I dunno what—"

"I don't care. It's fine. Listen. If Hannah's not with you, I think the stalker took her."

"Oh, oh shit. She *was* with me. She went to the bathroom, but—I'll look for her."

"Go," demanded Luke.

Luke cursed as the next light ahead of him turned red. He had almost caught up to the BMW, which also stopped at a red light just a block away. He kept the phone pressed to his ear, watching for the lights to his left to turn yellow. The crosswalk indicator counted down. *9. 8. 7. 6.*

The lights a block ahead turned green first, and the BMW turned left. Before Luke could follow, it was out of sight.

Luke flew into the intersection as soon as the opposing lights turned red. He couldn't waste a second. He turned a block later to follow the BMW, but it was nowhere in sight. Still, Luke had an idea where it was going.

"I can't find her," Adam said, panic taking over his drunken voice. "What do we do?"

"Call the cops. Send them to the pier. She's in danger."

When Luke got to the pier, he spotted the BMW in the parking lot. That was the good news. The bad news: a boat was just pulling away from the dock.

He rushed to the nearest rental office. Closed. Of course they wouldn't be open. Luke found an after-hours emergency number posted near the door and dialled it.

"James Bay Rentals, what's the emergency?"

"I need a boat," Luke said. "Can you send someone?"

"I'm sorry, sir. Rentals are closed until tomorrow. This line is for existing—"

"Look, I—someone is in danger, and I need a boat now. Please."

"What sort of danger, sir?"

Luke flexed his fingers on his free hand. "Someone's been kidnapped, and he just took her out on the water. I need to follow him."

"Have you contacted the police? The coast guard?"

"Someone's called the police. Do you have the number for the coast guard?"

"Yes, sir. Are you ready to take it down?"

Luke memorized the number and called it immediately. Hopefully they wouldn't be too late.

CHAPTER FIFTY-FOUR

Hannah woke up feeling nauseous and disoriented. Her head pounded. She went to cradle it with her hands, but she felt a sharp tug at her wrists as she pulled. She realized her hands were hand-cuffed to a chair.

She started to panic. She didn't know where she was. It was dark, and all she could hear was a deep hum. She was confused and scared. She breathed in quick, short breaths. It felt like her heart was going to beat out of her chest. She was soaked in sweat, and tears began to stream down her face.

She tried to calm herself. She knew that her body could not sustain the panic and that she would have to calm down.

She realized the room was rocking. She was on the water. She was on a boat.

She tried to remember how she got there. She could barely remember anything. The last thing she remembered was getting to the party with Adam. She wondered if she had been drugged.

"*Hello?*" she shouted. "Can anybody hear me?"

She was desperate. She strained and wriggled to try to reach her phone in her pocket, but it was no use. She mashed her thigh against the chair's armrest. If only she could activate the voice dialer, she could call for help.

Occasionally, Hannah could swear she heard faint mutterings, but then the silence would take over. The voice—who was it talking to?

When her adrenaline high ebbed, Hannah fell in and out of consciousness. There must have still been drugs in her system, and the alcohol only made things worse.

Fighting her exhaustion, Hannah opened her eyes a crack. She saw Hunter. She couldn't believe her eyes. It was Hunter, not Aidan—she was sure of it. Her very own brother, standing before her eyes. She wondered how he had gotten here. How was he alive?

She tried to touch his face, but her hands were stuck. She had forgotten about the cuffs. Her mouth was dry, and she couldn't speak.

Hunter was bleeding from a deep gash in his forehead. Hunter looked Hannah in the eyes and moved closer to her. He looked sullen. Defeated.

"He's coming for you, Hannah. He's coming for you the same way he came for me."

She heard a loud thud and opened her eyes. Hunter was gone, and the lights in the cabin practically blinded her. As her eyes adjusted and she regained control of her eyelids, she saw a figure by the door.

Aidan.

CHAPTER FIFTY-FIVE

It was him. Aidan walked up and stood in front of her, casting a shadow over her face. She knew this wasn't a dream. He had come for her, just like her brother had warned would happen. All this time, he was after her. Toying with her. She wondered what would drive him to do this—to harm his own family.

He looked her in the eyes and smiled. His smile disgusted her. She wanted to get away, but a part of her knew that she likely would not leave this boat alive. She would end up just like her brother. A corpse floating in the water. A soul lost to the sea.

Aidan shook his head slowly. "Really, Hannah? Adam again? You know, you've been *really* hard to get alone lately."

"What do you want, Aidan?" Hannah's mouth felt like rubber as she forced the words out.

"You do remember! So the video worked. Thank *God*. I was really hurt when you mistook me for Hunter. We look nothing alike. And he's dead, obviously."

Aidan grinned, revealing his single dimple. "You should know what I want. A family. You. It's all I've ever wanted. I tried to make Hunter understand, but he was so—so *thick*. I didn't want to hurt him. He just wouldn't listen, and, well, I got a little carried away. Couldn't very well return the tender to the cruise ship with an unconscious man bleeding all over the place. So I cracked an egg. You have to, sometimes. You know, to make an omelette.

"And besides, he deserved what he got. Hot-shot doctor, thinking he's better than me. Well, *he* put me where I ended up. *He* separated us—cut me out of the family."

"You're sick," Hannah said. "And I'm a doctor too."

"And I'm so proud of you! I've had an eye on you for a while, you know. My little sister. So successful. You're too dependent on men, though. I thought you were doing so well until you met that Luke character. And then straight from him, on to Adam? We don't want those old habits coming back. I'll look out for you. Now that we've moved Hunter's things out, we can live together. Never be apart."

Adam, Hannah thought. *He'll notice me missing. I just need to live through this. They'll find me.*

Hannah knew she needed to stay on Aidan's good side, but her thoughts were still a mess. There were too many things she had to know, and this might have been her only chance to learn the answers. She blurted out the first question in her head.

"Why did you take pages from Hunter's diary?"

"Hm. So you noticed, did you? Unlucky." Aidan pulled another chair in front of her and sat, holding one knee in his hands. He leaned back and looked down at her. "He was a little dramatic, wasn't he? Couldn't have you reading all that and getting the wrong idea. Not without proper context, anyway." He narrowed his eyes at her. "How much of those pages did you read?"

"None. I didn't—I just noticed the pages were cut. It looked like there should have been more."

Hannah knew she wasn't a very good liar, so she quickly changed the subject. Her mind went to the postcard he had put in her luggage. "How did you know about the Black Forest?"

Aidan lowered his head and exhaled sharply. Hannah started to regret asking.

"I knew about everything the rest of you did without me. Mom and Dad still spoke to me—for a while. Not that I care anymore. They're dead to me. Dad sold me down the river, and the both of them only really cared about Hunter anyway. You know they barely mentioned you when we reconnected? All they could talk about was Hunter. Well, we don't need any of them. You and me, Hannah. All we need is each other."

Hannah had to restrain herself from exploding in fury. She didn't have to for long. A faint, flashing blue light coming in through the open door had caught her attention.

The change in Hannah's expression hadn't escaped Aidan's notice. He stood and turned, knocking his chair over. "What did you do?" he demanded. "How did they find us?"

"I didn't do anything! I wouldn't!" said Hannah desperately.

Hannah's head whipped to the side, and she felt a wave of pain from one side of her face. Her jaw ached. She tasted blood.

Aidan rubbed his knuckles. "You're not a liar. Don't. Lie." He pulled a duffel bag from a closet and fished out a rope and a roll of duct tape. Then, he tore off a piece of tape and brought it to Hannah's mouth.

"No!" Hannah shouted, but that was all she could get out before he clamped her jaw shut and taped her lips tight. When she continued to struggle and whimper through the tape, he wound a second strip around her head for good measure.

"I didn't want it to come to this, but you gave me no choice. They won't let me leave here a free man, and I'm not getting locked up again." He started tying Hannah's legs together. "Luckily, I came prepared. We're going out the way our brother did. That'll teach Mom and Dad, won't it?"

Hannah screamed through her nose. There were so many things she regretted. She looked back on her life and wondered where everything had gone so wrong. She wondered if things would be different if she had paid more attention—if she had asked more questions.

He uncuffed one of her hands from the chair and grabbed her wrist forcefully. Hannah winced in pain as he tugged the loose cuff and locked it around his own wrist.

Aidan jerked her up from the chair and threw her over his shoulder. She tried to fight and kick, but she was too weak. Hannah struggled to breathe through her nose, but the tape constricted one of her nostrils. She wondered how much worse drowning would be. She hoped it would be quick.

In the last seconds as Aidan carried her through the door and out onto the deck, Hannah thought about Luke. Aidan had tried to make her think that Luke was someone she couldn't trust. The entire time, Luke had been trying to protect her. She wished she had tried harder to hear him out. She knew it must have been difficult for him to have witnessed her brother's death. She knew that he probably saw Hunter every time he looked at her.

"You know, Hannah . . . I really thought you and I could be close. I thought we would meet, and you would realize how much we have in common—how similar we are." His words made her sick. They shared blood, but nothing else. She could never find it in herself to kill her own brother.

Aidan carried her to the edge of the boat as she pleaded through the tape. She begged, but she knew there was no point. She knew his mind was made up. The moment she had looked him in the eyes up close, she could see that there was no good inside him. He was broken in a way that could never be fixed.

The police boat had almost caught up to them, but they were too late. Aidan gripped her tight and sat on the handrail.

"See you on the other side, Hannah."

Hannah saw one more flash of blue light before they plunged into the ocean. The water burned her entire body. It was so cold, and every cut and bruise on her body ached in excruciating pain. There was nothing she could do. She tried to squirm and fight her way out of the ropes, cuffs, and Aidan's arms. Her body moved on its own as her survival instincts kicked in.

Eventually, she stopped fighting. She knew there was no hope. As the last of her air escaped through her nose, Hannah closed her eyes and tried to find peace. She thought about Luke again and how grateful she was to have met him. She thought about her parents and how they gave her a wonderful childhood. Most of all, she thought of Hunter: the one person in the world who always understood her and always would. The two of them were bonded so deeply that even death could not separate them.

Hannah craned her neck to the sky as her body forced her to inhale a lungful of water. The blue light from the surface faded, and everything went black. She knew it was time for her to leave this earth for good and join her brother.

An overwhelming wave of white light flooded her vision. And with that, she was gone.

CHAPTER FIFTY-SIX

"Hannah."

"Hannah, open your eyes."

"Hannah, it's me. Open your eyes. You're going to be alright."

The voice was faint; she couldn't make out who it was. For a moment she was convinced it was Hunter.

She wondered if she was dead. She had never thought about what the afterlife would be like. Would she be stuck forever in a static state of nothingness? Would she hear her brother call for her and never be able to reach him or see his face?

Her body was shaking. An image started to appear, and she realized with overwhelming relief that the man with the green eyes was sitting above her, cradling her head. With great effort, she lifted her arm touched his face. He leaned in towards her and hugged her close. He kissed her as a tear rolled down his face.

"How did you find me?" Hannah worried that none of this was real. She wondered if all of this was a dream she was encountering in death. Her chest ached, but the pain didn't matter to her.

"I was watching the party, and I saw his car leaving in a hurry. I couldn't catch him." Luke sounded like he felt he had let her down. He held her hands in his.

"I thought I lost you, Hannah." Luke rubbed his fingers over the red scrapes on her wrists. She could see the concern in his eyes. She hated that she brought him into all of this. He deserved better, and she wished that he could have a normal life.

"What about Aidan?" Hannah hated the sound of his name coming out of her mouth.

The look Hannah saw on his face was the definition of pure hatred.

"Your brother? He's alive. They're taking him in another ambulance. You won't have to see him again until his trial."

"Trial?"

Luke's face showed patience behind the anger. "Attempted murder-suicide, for one. Kidnapping. And we'll get him on Hunter's murder before we're done with him. But none of that matters now, Hannah. You're safe, and he can't hurt you anymore."

Relief finally sunk in as Hannah relaxed and stared up at the ambulance ceiling.

"How did you know I would be at that party?" Hannah asked.

"I've been keeping an eye on you since your flight landed." Luke was calm and warm in his tone, but she could see in his eyes that he felt betrayed by her.

"I'm sorry, Luke. I wanted to move on. I wanted things to be normal again." She felt ashamed as she said the words. He hadn't deserved to watch her carry on with Adam.

Luke turned his head and nodded gravely. Hannah could feel the space between them widening. This man had saved her life, but she couldn't change what she had done to him. She struggled to find the words that could make things better. The ones she found weren't enough, but it was a start.

"Thank you, Luke."

Luke leaned in and kissed her. His lips were soft. She had missed his smell.

"I love you so much, Hannah." The words came out in a whisper—like a soft breeze of the wind blowing through her hair.

Hannah knew that without Hunter things would never be the

same. She knew that she would need to move on. She knew that's what Hunter would have wanted.

EPILOGUE

Three months later.

Hannah ran quickly through the sand. Her legs felt particularly heavy that day. She ran for miles with the sun shining down on her, warming her entire body. She breathed in the fresh air, smelled the aroma of the ocean, and watched as the clouds moved through the sky, the sun peeking in and out to greet her.

Even there, on the Atlantic beaches of La Rochelle, some habits never died.

Luke had protested when Hannah told him of her plans. He wanted to be near her, he said. He couldn't stand to lose her again—even for a little while. But Hannah had to consider what *she* wanted.

At that moment, she wanted to travel.

In a way, Aidan had been right. She had been too dependent on the men in her life. When it wasn't Hunter, it would be someone else—but it was always the same. Hannah didn't want for things to be the same anymore. She had sacrificed too much in trying to keep it that way.

Luke would still be there when she went home—if she wanted to be with him. But it would be her choice.

She would decide.

10435911R00127

Made in the USA
Lexington, KY
27 September 2018